Pack Train

Scott Bailey's first day with a US Government pack train very nearly becomes his last day on earth. Narrowly escaping an ambush, he soon experiences other attempts on his life. Someone is determined to kill him but he does not know who or why. He finds himself embroiled in a dangerous situation involving law officers, military men and renegades and suspects that he is being used as bait to trap the leader of a criminal operation.

Scott begins to unravel the mystery after being given some vital information by the new friends he is making in town. He teams up with Maley, a government investigator with a dubious reputation. They work together to destroy the criminal operation but the unknown leader remains at large. It all leads up to a final life-and-death confrontation in which Scott discovers that the only person he can trust is himself. . . .

By the same author

Outlaw Vengeance
Warbonnet Creek
Red Rock Crossing
Killer's Kingdom
Range Rustlers
Track Down the Devil
Comanche Country
The Raiders
Murdering Wells
Hard Road to Holford
Crooked Foot's Gold
Breakout
Domingo's Trail
Crooked Creek

Pack Train

Greg Mitchell

A Black Horse Western

ROBERT HALE · LONDON

© Greg Mitchell 2015
First published in Great Britain 2015

ISBN 978-0-7198-1563-8

Robert Hale Limited
Clerkenwell House
Clerkenwell Green
London EC1R 0HT

www.halebooks.com

Falkirk Council	
Askews & Holts	2015
AF	£13.99

Typeset by
Derek Doyle & Associates, Shaw Heath
Printed and bound in Great Britain by
CPI Antony Rowe, Chippenham and Eastbourne

ONE

'So you reckon you know all about mule packing?' Rafe Gilmore asked. He had to be sure; his eyes, beneath their bushy grey eyebrows, narrowed and the lines on his seamed forehead grew deeper in a questioning frown. Unconsciously his fingers combed his short, grey beard.

The young man before him looked strong enough and he had a casually efficient look about him, but the US Army was particular about the civilian contractors who kept them supplied in the field. Not all out-of-work cowhands were good packers.

'I didn't say I knew it all,' Scott Bailey corrected. 'I've packed mules before, can tie a diamond hitch and a squaw hitch and know a lash rope from a sling rope, but I'm used to sawbuck pack saddles, not the army type. I reckon there are a few tricks of the trade that I'll need to pick up. What I don't know, I can soon learn.'

'How do you go with mules? A lot of folks don't

seem to get on with them. And they can kick too – so fast that you don't know which end got you.'

'I know that and there are a few horses damn near as fast. A mule is like any other animal, treat them decent and you don't have too many worries. You need to stay on your guard, though, if you're working with some that are naturally mean or have been made sour.'

The big contractor seemed happy with that reply and continued, 'I'm warning you, young fellow. It's heavy work. Uncle Sam likes at least two hundred pounds on his mules and you could find yourself supporting as much as your own weight until it can be secured to a pack saddle. Sometimes too you might need to be on the downhill side of a slipping pack and have to lift high. The work is easier for tall men like yourself, but it still takes a lot of muscle. The job's yours if you want it. You can start as a second-class packer at thirty dollars a month and found. In a year or so you might make it to first class, if you stay around that long.'

'I'll take any job I can get at present. When do I start work?'

'Be at the army supply depot tomorrow at five a.m. It's that long building you can see on the other side of the mule corral. You're in luck as the main part of this pack train is with the cavalry at Fort Harris, but this detachment has been stationed in Crossville near a depot supplying some infantry posts that are easy to reach from here. There's a chance our operation might be returned to Fort Harris later, but I expect it will be here for a while. You'll have an easy start tomorrow, just a two-day round trip taking supplies up to some army posts in the Big Pine hills. They have half a company of the Ninth Infantry and a couple of signal stations up there keeping an eye on the back of the Cheyenne reservation. Sometimes those red varmints sneak out and raise a bit of hell around the place.'

'Have they ever attacked a pack train?' Scott asked.

'Not around here they haven't. It's too close to home. We have never had any Indian trouble here in Crossville. Now don't forget – be at the depot at five o'clock.' With that instruction, the big contractor turned and walked away, an untidy figure in a rumpled suit: an outdoorsman masquerading unsuccessfully as a town-dweller.

It was still dark when Scott made his way to the supply depot. He was dismayed to see, by the light of a couple of lanterns, that the mules were already loaded and three men were waiting. One was a short man in a military overcoat, somewhere in his forties with a neat moustache and goatee beard. His companion was a tall man in a buckskin suit with a six-shooter belted around his waist. The lantern light showed a face almost as dark as an Indian and that face wore a scowl. Scott wondered if he had misjudged the time and was late. The third man was a tall, skinny, untidy individual who was not standing with the others and who seemed to be shivering uncontrollably. He was leaning against a saddled mule with a blindfold draped over one arm. He also wore a large revolver and had a canvas army cartridge belt strapped around his waist.

'I'm Scott Bailey. It looks like I'm late.'

The dark man's serious face relaxed a little. 'You ain't late. I'm standing in for Gilmore, the name's Lije Jarrett. This is Lieutenant Cowell. He runs the depot and that sick-looking customer propping up the mule is Ed Newton. He'll be running things on this trip. He had a few too many drinks last night, but couldn't sleep. He turned up early and wanted to get on the road. He was too drunk to help much with the loading, but helped by a couple of volunteers, we got the mules loaded. We thought we'd give you a good start on your first day. Corporal Wade handles most of the records and stuff. He works over there in the office, you can catch up with him when you get back. It's a pity you missed seeing how things are done, but Ed will show you over the next couple of days. It won't take you long to learn.'

'I hope not and I sure appreciate the easy start,' Scott said. He had not expected such consideration.

Jarrett made a dismissive gesture. 'We figured it was the least we could do, sending a new man out with Ed. You might find that he's not a lot of help while he's in this condition. Rafe was going to fire him, but has decided to give him one more chance. He's a damn good packer when he's sober, so watch what he does and do as he says. I'll leave you two to

8

get acquainted. Your saddle and carbine are over by the corral and your riding mule is the grey one in the corral.'

'What's the need for a carbine? I have my Colt six-shooter and you reckon we won't have Indian trouble.'

The lieutenant explained. 'Army packers are all given a Springfield carbine and a cartridge belt holding forty rounds. Sometimes packers have been involved in skirmishes with Indians. It won't happen here, but you carry the carbine when on army business. It's free and Uncle Sam does not give away all that much, so take it and don't argue. I'll see you back here tomorrow night. Good luck.'

Scott walked over to where Ed was still leaning against his mule. He introduced himself and the packer extended a shaky hand. As though each word was causing him great pain, the packer mumbled, 'Pleased to meet you. Get your mule saddled up and we can be on our way. It's gonna be a rough couple of hours – I wonder how sick a man needs to be before he dies.'

The grey mule was quiet and Scott soon had the mule driver's Morgan saddle in place. He adjusted the stirrups to his own length, buckled the extra cartridge belt around his waist and rigged a temporary sling for his carbine across the pommel. Then he led his mount over to where Ed was waiting.

The packer's instructions were simple. First Scott had to help his companion into the saddle and then hand him the lead rope of an unsaddled mule mare wearing a bell. Ed mumbled that the mules would all follow the one with the bell so all Scott had to do was unhitch the other mules and ride along behind to keep an eye out for any packs that might shift.

'I didn't rig these packs and there's a chance that some haven't been set right. A crooked pack needs fixin' pronto or it can wreck a mule's back. Keep a close eye on them and call me if you see something coming loose. But please – don't call too loud just in case my head drops off.'

They left Crossville just as day was breaking with Ed clinging to his saddle horn while the mules dutifully followed the one who was leading.

Scott found that after a horse, his mount sometimes felt a little heavy on the bit, but had a brisk, comfortable walk. It was a pace that a mule could maintain all day even when heavily loaded and this was why the hybrids were so popular for pack work. He settled back to enjoy the ride and the new scenery that the rising sun revealed.

An hour's ride from town, they came to a small creek. Ed suddenly halted the train and mumbled, 'Let these critters have a drink. There're a lot of miles between this and the next water. Watch that none of them try to roll with the pack.'

After giving these instructions, Newton dismounted, lay down on the stream bank and immersed his head in the water. He was about to shake the water from his long hair, but remembered his headache just in time and instead let the water run down his shirt collar. As if trying to convince himself, he said to Scott, 'That sure feels better.'

'Glad to hear it. You were looking right poorly there for a while. How far are we going today?'

'By the time we drop off our full load at the three different posts it will be about twenty-five miles. That's just about the army's daily limit for mules carrying two hundred pounds.'

'What are we taking to these posts? These mules are strolling along as though they are not carrying much weight at all.'

Ed tried to ignore his misery and groaned, 'Who cares? Winter's comin' on and some of those loads look like bales of blankets. They ain't very heavy. Them sharp-cornered boxes showin' under the pack covers could be bacon, or hard bread, or even ammunition. There's always coffee, salt, sugar and canned goods as well. As long as we keep the packs in place and deliver the stuff, I don't care two hoots about what we are carryin'.'

Scott indicated the steeply rising ridges to the west. 'Are they where we're going?'

'Yeah, in another mile or so we start workin' our way up them slopes. The trail's steep, but not too bad except for where there's been an old landslide about halfway up. Mules can get across it, though we need to be careful. The slope on the downhill side is pretty steep. You don't want to go for a slide down there.

One more thing, you could load that carbine you're carryin'. There's grizzlies on that mountain and they have been known to attack mules if they have cubs about. But don't shoot unless you have to. I don't think my head could stand all that noise today. Now we'd best be on our way again while I'm still fightin' the temptation just to lie here and die.'

They started the ascent, working along the side of the hills on a path that gradually became steeper. As the train went higher Scott found that he could see above the belt of pines on the lower slopes to the rolling grasslands that were part of the Cheyenne reservation. It was easy to see why the army had established the observation posts where they had, although at night, to his way of thinking, they would be of little value.

The trail wound around the contours of the hills. Sometimes he could see Ed riding in front while at other times he would be out of sight around a bend, but the tinkling of the lead mule's bell indicated where he was.

It was easy to recognize the landslide when they reached it, a wide swathe of bare earth and rocks that had carried away trees and part of the trail. There was room for the nimble-footed mules to pass, but the steep slope on the downhill side looked grim and unforgiving, although it was only about a hundred yards wide. He could see that Ed had reached safe footing when his own mule started to pick its way across. He was watching where the mule was walking when a volley of gunfire erupted from the slopes above.

Almost disbelieving, he saw Ed throw up his arms and fall from his mount. Grey powder smoke was spurting from the bushes on the hillside, but before Scott could even see the attackers or raise the carbine he was carrying, his mule collapsed and toppled off the trail.

TWO

He hit the ground with a force that almost knocked the wind out of him. He felt the sharp stones he had landed on before he started to slide down the slope in a cascade of dust and pebbles. His first thought as he tumbled and rolled was for the whereabouts of the mule; a flailing kick or having it fall on top of him could prove fatal and momentarily he forgot the men and the guns. Then to his great relief he discovered that the mule was ahead of him.

His first reaction was to dig the butt of the carbine he still held into the earth to stop his descent, but he realized that if he did this he would then be exposed on open ground. It was safer to endure the pummelling descent while the dust cloud offered some protection. Finally he rolled over some young pine trees that were starting to grow on the slope and hit hard against a log that had been carried downhill years before. Bruised, gravel-rashed and only half comprehending what had happened, he came to a halt.

By sheer good fortune he found himself hidden from view. The young trees had sprung up behind him and screened him from the attackers while the dust he had collected gave him the same colour as the earth around him. Dazed though he was, Scott knew that he would not be ignored by those who had fired on him.

He had hunted often enough to know that movement attracts attention so he lay still and let the dust settle around him. A doubt existed that he might be visible from above, but could only hope that he was not. Afraid to move or look back up the slope, he kept his face in the dirt and hoped that the attackers would not come looking for him. He suspected that Ed had been killed and was sure that the killers would prefer not to leave behind any witnesses.

They were strangely quiet with no triumphant war cries to indicate that the attackers were Indians, although given the proximity to the reservation, this had to be a possibility.

He heard the bell on the leading mule and knew that the loaded animals were being taken away. Fervently hoping that the killers would go with them, he began planning his own escape from the scene. But then a man's voice from up on the trail dashed his hopes.

'There were two of them. The one behind looked like he was shot, but we have to make sure. McComb, go down to the bottom of the slide and make sure he's dead. Then catch up with us straight away.'

Scott waited until he could scarcely hear the mule bell fading as the train was led away and cautiously raised his head. Nobody was on the raw earth of the slide. Apparently the killers knew an easier way to get around it. He took a chance and climbed to his feet. Hoping that he had been unobserved, he crept clear of the base of the slide and crawled into a nearby thicket. Screened by berry bushes, he removed his bandanna and began to wipe dust from the carbine's breech and sights.

He had not seen which side of the landslide his would-be killer had taken and could only watch, swivelling his eyes from one side to the other, fearful that even a slight movement of his head would be seen. A few minutes later, he heard a horse forcing its way through the brush. The man was coming from his right side.

Cocking the carbine before the horse was close enough to hear the sound, Scott waited, feeling the hair rise on the back of his neck. Never in his life had he shot at another human being, but he knew that he had to kill this one if he wanted to live.

The horse came closer and soon a flicker of movement was seen among the trees. Every step the animal took brought its rider into clearer view. Scott lined up his sights and waited.

McComb was expecting to find his man dead or seriously wounded but had drawn his revolver as a safety precaution. Even that was of little help.

Scott placed his front sight on the centre of the red undershirt showing under the man's open buckskin jacket. Shutting out all thoughts of what he was about to do, he squeezed the trigger. At close range the military carbine had considerable power and the heavy bullet flipped McComb over the rump of his pony. He hit the ground in an untidy sprawl with the gun flying from his hand. The frightened pony wheeled about and fled.

Scott drew his revolver and bounded forward. McComb was on his back, his fingers clawing at the loose earth and his shirt front already a mass of blood. For a brief moment, he stared wide-eyed at the man who had shot him, but then he gave a choking sound and fell back. The life was gone from his still-open eyes.

Briefly Scott was elated to think that he had survived the encounter, but then the doubts began to creep in. Should he have killed the man? What if he had just captured and disarmed him and taken his horse? Then he remembered the horse and realized that it had escaped him and he was on foot with an unknown number of McComb's friends not far away. They would have heard the shot.

There was no time to lose. Reloading the carbine, he set off trotting through the forest at the base of the hill. It would be a while before McComb was missed and he wanted to be as far away as possible before the others came searching.

He travelled parallel to the road, staying in the trees downhill from it. The ground was rough underfoot, but he dared not seek the easier walking of the trail. It would be too easy for the hunters to find him. He soon felt the effects of the heat and unaccustomed exercise and panting heavily, sought a shady spot to rest for a few minutes. It was lucky that he did.

A flash of white on a painted pony caught his eye and Scott froze. They were moving through the trees riding single-file in almost complete silence, four Indian warriors and they were passing in front of him, about forty yards away. He feared that one would look sideways, but none did. The leader was peering intently ahead and the others were watching him. The first brave pointed silently and Scott knew they were heading for the ambush site. Were they part of the ambush or were they merely attracted by the gunshots? For all he knew they could have been searching for him.

Minutes dragged by and Scott begrudged every second he was forced to wait, but he had to be sure that the Indians were out of earshot before he resumed his journey. He started again with a little less pace, but a lot more vigilance. The four he saw might not have been the only Indians in the vicinity and it was vital that he saw them before they saw him. Hot, exhausted and with nerves stretched to breaking point, he finally reached the place where the mule trail met the road to Crossville.

Another surprise awaited him there although this

time it was a pleasant one.

A buckboard had stopped in the shade and he saw two ladies standing near the horses' heads. They looked up in horror at the dirty figure that emerged from the brush.

One lady was small and young, early twenties at most. She wore a man's hat over her long, dark hair, a green jacket and a brown divided skirt. She had been studying a broken rein until Scott appeared.

Her companion was taller, possibly slightly older with red hair. This one wore a more feminine straw hat and her long dress was covered by a grey linen duster. She moved closer to the buckboard and Scott suspected that a weapon of some kind might have been there.

Both women looked startled and to allay their suspicions, Scott stopped and removed his hat. 'Good afternoon, ladies. I'm Scott Bailey, an army mule packer. There's been some bad trouble on the trail and I am wondering if you could give me a ride back to Crossville.'

'What sort of trouble?' the tall redhead demanded suspiciously.

'I was with a pack train that was attacked on the trail to Big Pine hills. My partner was killed. Whoever attacked us knows that I've escaped and could be fairly close behind. We all need to get out of here as quick as we can.'

The smaller, dark-haired one looked startled by the news and then frowned as she held up a broken rein. 'We can't go anywhere until this rein is fixed. I tried knotting it but that won't work. It keeps coming undone.'

Mainly to free his hands, but partially to offer reassurance, Scott passed his carbine to the tall redhead. 'If you'll hold this for me, ma'am. I can soon fix that.'

Surprised, the tall one held the carbine as she would a snake. 'Is this thing loaded?'

'Sure is, but it's safe the way it is. It might be a good idea too if you keep looking up the trail. If there's trouble on the way it's best we know about it as soon as possible.'

Taking out his sharp pocket knife, Scott rounded the ends of the broken rein and cut a slot in each piece. Then by looping the ends through the slots, he made a neat join in the leather. 'That's fixed it and the join won't break. It will hold until you get to Crossville. Now I would appreciate a lift, but I can understand it if you are a bit wary of a disreputable character with a wild story. In that case, I'd appreciate your calling at the army stores depot and saying that Scott Bailey needs help, Ed Newton has been killed and the pack train stolen.'

The younger girl smiled and told him, 'It might be best that you deliver the message yourself, Mister Bailey. Jump on to the tray and we can get started. Joan, you had best give the man back his gun. I don't think this is a good place to hang around.'

Joan, needing no urging to thrust the carbine

back into Scott's hands, hurried to the passenger's side of the buckboard. The other girl reattached the mended rein and climbed into the driver's seat.

Scott glanced back as he seated himself in the baggage tray. He could see a fair way back along the trail and his eye caught movement. The tiny figures of riders were coming into view at a point where the trees did not obstruct his view of the trail.

'Best if we get going, ladies. I can see some riders about half a mile back.'

Joan asked in a voice tinged with anxiety, 'Are they Indians?'

'They're too far away to tell,' Scott told her. 'But whoever they are, you don't want to meet them.'

THREE

The younger girl shook the reins, called to the horses and started them off at their usual rate of a sedate trot. Then she repeated her urgings and the team increased their pace.

The buckboard had springs, but the occupants were bounced about on the rutted dirt road. Scott was forced to hold the back of the seat to avoid being shaken out of the vehicle. The long plume of dust behind them obscured his view and he was not sure if they were still being pursued and felt it was best not to take chances. With great difficulty he adjusted the carbine's rear sight to four hundred yards. Bouncing around as he was, he knew that accurate shooting was out of the question, but clung to the faint hope that a shot might discourage the pursuit.

They surged through the shallow ford where the pack train had watered that morning, sending up a shower of spray as the wheels bumped over the stony bottom. Another moment and they were on smoother ground again. Now there were only a couple of miles between them and safety.

Away from the shelter of the mountains a drifting wind carried the dust off the trail and, for the first time, Scott could see back along the route. The riders were no longer there. The contour of the land precluded the possibility that they were taking a short cut and he could only guess that their proximity to town might have discouraged them.

'Ma'am,' he called above the noise of their progress, 'you can slow down. Those riders are not following. You can save those horses for a bit. No point in running the daylights out of them if it isn't needed.'

The team needed no urging to decrease the pace and were happy to drop back to a trot. The run had taken its toll on their energy.

Joan looked back and asked Scott, 'Are you sure they're gone?'

'No doubt about it. We're close enough to town now and there's no way they could get around us and cut us off at this distance. It's lucky for me that you ladies came along when you did.'

'I think it was lucky for us all that Mary is such a good driver. I really thought we would have an accident at the speed we were going.'

So, her name is Mary, Scott told himself, she is quite a girl.

The first buildings in Crossville soon came into view. There were not many of them, strung out on both sides of a single street.

'Where should we let you off?' Mary called back over her shoulder.

'I reckon I should go to the army supply depot. It's that long building with the corrals that you can see ahead on the left. I'm mighty obliged to you ladies. Do you mind if I ask who you are?'

'I'm Joan McRae, my husband has recently bought the general store in Crossville,' the red-haired one announced.

'I'm Mary Hegarty. My father just sold the store. He has taken up a smallholding on the other side of town. I was just showing Mrs McRae around.'

'I'm sure glad you came along. Things were looking pretty bad for me back there.'

Not much happened in Crossville and the sight of the two ladies, their bedraggled passenger and foam-covered horses attracted every eye as they moved down the street.

They stopped in front of the stores depot and Scott climbed down. 'I'm sorry to involve you ladies in this,' he said, 'but there's been a murder and a robbery so you might be asked about what you saw later.'

Joan McRae smiled. 'Don't worry about it. I thought this town might be a little dull. Now I have a story I can tell my grandchildren, if I ever have any. We might see you around town sometime.'

Scott watched the buckboard turn away as he unloaded the carbine. When he turned he saw Lije

Jarrett hurrying towards him. 'Bailey, what in the hell are you doing back here? What's happened?'

'The train was ambushed at that landslide place. I reckon Ed's dead. I got away, but the killers came after me. If those ladies hadn't picked me up on the road, I guess I would have been killed too.'

'Was it Indians?'

'Could have been. I saw some after the ambush, but I know there were at least two white men involved.'

Jarrett looked at him sharply. 'How do you know that?'

'Because I heard one send someone named McComb after me, but I got him instead. Do you know anyone by that name?'

Jarrett thought for a second or two. 'It's familiar,' he admitted. 'I seem to have heard it around town somewhere, though I can't put a face to it.'

'You'd better come with me and tell the lieutenant and Rafe Gilmore what happened. The sheriff and the army will both need to know too.'

They called first at Gilmore's office, a small shed built on to the side of a barn. Their boss was seated at a desk sorting through an untidy pile of papers. 'Bailey,' he said in surprise, 'what are you doing here?'

'The pack train was ambushed. I only got away because my mule was shot and fell off the trail with me. I reckon Ed's been killed, but I couldn't see from where I was.'

'You mean you left Ed without checking on him?' Jarrett's attitude had suddenly changed from a sympathizer to an accuser. 'What if he's lying out there badly wounded? How can you be sure he's dead?'

Bailey was in no mood to tolerate Jarrett's sudden change of mood as he suspected that it might have been caused by a desire to impress Gilmore. 'I'm sure that Ed would be finished because those same murdering polecats sent a man to find me and finish me off. I was in no position to help Ed.'

'I can understand that,' Gilmore said. 'Where did it happen?'

'At a place on the trail where there had been a big landslide. I think they got Ed as he came round a bend in the trail. They must have fired at me from somewhere above the landslide, but killed my mule instead. It fell down the landslide with me.'

'Are you hurt?'

'I'm scratched and bruised and will probably feel like hell tomorrow, but I think I got out of it pretty lightly.'

Gilmore looked hard at him as if assessing how truthful he had been about his condition. Then he said, 'Would you be up to taking a party up to the ambush site tomorrow?'

'I reckon so. Do I still have a job after that?'

'I don't see why not. Now let's go and see Cowell. He'll need to know what happened. Lije, will you see Sheriff Hennessey and let him know the situation. No doubt he'll want to stick his bib in.'

26

They walked around the mule corrals to the supply depot, a long, barn-like structure with a couple of empty wagons parked outside. Gilmore knocked on a small side door and called, 'It's Rafe Gilmore, Lieutenant. I have some bad news for you.'

The door opened almost immediately and there was Cowell, hatless and coatless, clutching a large ledger of some kind and a pencil. Seated at a desk was a young, dark-haired man with a corporal's stripes on the sleeve of his uniform jacket. His eyes widened as he saw Scott, but the officer asked all the questions. Once again the new packer had to explain why he was not up in the Big Pine hills.

'Are you saying that they took the entire pack train?'

'I don't know, but it seems most likely. I was in no position to check on anything.'

Rafe interjected. 'I think we need to get up there fast just in case Ed got away or is lying wounded somewhere in the brush. I'm going to get a few men together and we'll take a ride up there tomorrow. I am a bit worried, though. If the attackers were Cheyenne they might be waiting for the next party to come across that landslide.'

Cowell told him, 'Those three observation posts keep in touch by heliograph and signal with lanterns, but Post Number One at the far end of the hills has a telegraph link to Fort Harris. I'll telegraph the fort and they can send orders to Post Number One to be relayed to Number Three, which is closest to the landslide. Number Three can send out a patrol to meet us at the landslide. I only have five men here at the depot but will bring two along with us tomorrow just to beef up the party a bit. Corporal Wade will run the place in my absence.'

'Go ahead and make your plans,' Rafe said. 'Right now I'm taking this man to the doctor to get him patched up. Then I will get him settled into our bunkhouse and hope he's fit enough to go out in the morning.'

'I'll be there tomorrow,' Scott declared. 'You can bet on that.'

Next morning he kept his word even if he had lost some of his enthusiasm. After being patched up by the doctor, he settled accounts at the boarding-house where he had been staying, collected his few possessions, moved them into the bunkhouse, and even bought a new shirt and pants with the advance Gilmore had given him on his pay. After a bath and a shave, he fell into a bunk and slept until Jarrett called him before daylight next morning. He was tired, stiff and sore, but felt slightly better after a hasty breakfast.

Jarrett indicated the saddle that Scott had brought with him. 'You might need that today. The government only allows fourteen riding saddles per pack train and half of ours are at Fort Harris with the rest of the outfit. We lost two yesterday and I'm not sure how many men are coming this morning. There's three soldiers coming, you and me and another packer called Bill Ruskin, who lives here in town. Sheriff Hennessey is sending one of his deputies and he'll probably have that old windbag, Dick Brannigan, with them but they'll have their own horses.'

'Who's Dick Brannigan?'

'He's an old squaw man. Like a lot of those old-timers, he claims to be an expert on Indians and tracking. Hennessey swears by him, but I doubt that he could track a buffalo through mud. I wouldn't put too much store in anything he says. He's like dozens of others around here, forever telling greenhorns about the number of Indians they killed but never venturing far from the saloons.'

'Is Gilmore coming?'

Jarrett shook his head. 'He changed his mind – I convinced him he's getting a bit too old to go traipsing about the mountains. I can find out all he needs to know.'

Scott had almost finished saddling his mule and was gently easing the cinch tighter when he saw the deputy and Brannigan arrive.

Tom Macklin, the deputy, was an average-looking man in his early thirties with a short, red beard and alert blue eyes that belied his almost leisurely manner of speaking. When introduced, Scott sensed that he was a man whose casual manner was carefully cultivated. He resolved to be guarded in his dealings with this one.

It was hard to guess Dick Brannigan's age as his

29

tanned, heavily lined face was mostly covered by an unruly grey beard. He wore a shapeless rag of a hat with a buckskin suit and moccasins and sat astride a roan Indian pony with split tips of its ears. He rode on an Indian chicken-snare saddle with a mangy bearskin cinched over it. His armaments were a Winchester repeater and ammunition belt which also supported a large knife in an Indian rawhide sheath, a fringed buckskin pouch and a holstered revolver the size of which indicated it was one of the varieties of the Colt Dragoon .44. If he was not an old mountain man, he certainly looked the part.

When Jarrett introduced them, Brannigan looked hard at him and chuckled. 'Sonny, you look like you've been fightin' wildcats so I reckon you'd be the one that got away yesterday.'

No prizes for guessing that, Scott thought, but almost immediately the humour went from Brannigan's face.

'Do you reckon there was injuns involved?'

'Can't say for sure. I heard one white man and shot another, but later I saw four Indians going through the brush towards where I came down.'

'So it could be white men with a few renegades?' asked Brannigan.

'It's possible, but I ain't in a position to say. Let's get up to where it all happened and maybe the tracks will tell you something.'

'They sure will, but it ain't always easy to tell some folks what they don't want to hear.'

'What wouldn't we want to hear?'

The old man looked mysterious. 'Just let's see what we find and then you might figure out the answer to your own question.'

FOUR

The party made good time with Jarrett, the lieutenant and Macklin riding in front and Brannigan,
Scott, Ruskin and the two mounted infantrymen following. They reached the landslide, approaching
cautiously until a group of blue-uniformed soldiers
called to them from the other side.

'Looks like there's nothing to worry about now,'
Cowell observed.

'And no tracks to read either,' Brannigan
mumbled under his breath to Scott. 'Damn fools
look like they've been walking all over the place.'

A bearded sergeant and four men were waiting for
them on the other side of the landslide. They had
marched from the signal station and announced to
Lieutenant Cowell that the road was clear.

To Scott's surprise, nobody seemed interested in
seeking his views as the only eyewitness of the attack.
The discovery of Ed's bullet-riddled body claimed
everyone's attention.

Brannigan dismounted, walked about for a while and returned to the others, shaking his head.

'He won't find anything – never does,' Scott heard Jarrett telling Cowell. The sudden shortening of the old man's stride and a fleeting angry look showed that he had heard the remark, but said nothing.

Addressing Macklin, the deputy, he announced, 'I can see where they took the mules down the hillside, headin' straight for the Cheyenne reservation.'

'I thought so,' Cowell announced. 'I'll signal for some cavalry to come from Fort Harris. They can ask a few questions from the Indian Agent and maybe arrest the ones concerned.'

'You could also trigger somethin' dangerous,' Brannigan interjected. 'This young fella here reckons there were white men involved. It's easy to lay a false trail towards the reservation and then sneak away in some other direction.'

'The cavalry will have proper scouts,' Jarrett said dismissively. 'They'll soon pick up those mule tracks. Now let's get Ed's body to the signal station and get him buried.'

The deputy had other ideas. 'No. We take him with us for the coroner. Just cover him up with some branches and we can pick him up as we go back to town.'

Then Macklin turned in his saddle and said to Brannigan, 'Dick, you and I might see if we can borrow Scott for a while and see what happened down there at the foot of the landslide. Sheriff

33

Hennessey insists that I cover all aspects of this crime and I don't reckon we'll learn much sitting here.'

'Glad to help,' Scott said, greatly relieved that someone was interested in his account.

Jarrett said sharply, 'You are not working for the sheriff, Bailey, and you won't go anywhere unless Lieutenant Cowell says so.'

'I'm sure the lieutenant won't object to my helping the law, seeing as how nobody else seems interested in what I know. It's all too easy just blaming it on the Indians.'

Jarrett's face darkened with anger. 'I'm representing Rafe Gilmore here and I say that you and Ruskin will do as you're told.'

The latter was all offended innocence and protested that he had no intention of going with the deputy. But Scott made his position clear.

'Gilmore can fire me later if he likes, but I'm taking the deputy down to where I shot McComb and you can't stop me.'

'Can't I?' Jarrett's hand moved closer to his gun butt.

'No you can't,' the deputy snapped angrily. 'If you make one move towards that gun, I'll kill you, and don't think I can't.'

'There's no need to take that attitude, Macklin.' Cowell was suddenly diplomatic. 'I'm sure that Lije wasn't meaning to threaten anyone. He was just looking after his boss's interests a little too zealously.'

'Glad to hear it.' The disbelief in the deputy's

voice was obvious. 'Now, Bailey, you take Dick down to where you shot this McComb character. I'll follow along here when I reckon it's safe to turn my back on Mr Jarrett.'

'Are you calling me a back-shooter?' Jarrett was livid with rage.

'I sure am. I recall arresting you for murder when a certain gambler in Crossville was shot in the back. You beat the charge, claiming self-defence though I still can't quite see how that could be. I think you had the best jury money could buy.'

'If you weren't wearing that star, I'd call you out for that. Maybe I should anyway.'

The click of a hammer being cocked claimed everyone's attention and they turned to see the army sergeant holding his long, Springfield .45/70. 'There's been enough shooting around here, but I'm prepared to fire one more shot at anyone who wants to stop the deputy from doing his job.'

'I'm in charge here, Sergeant,' Cowell said indignantly.

Still keeping his rifle trained on Jarrett, the sergeant said with complete insincerity. 'Sorry, sir. I just forgot for a moment.'

As the trio turned their mounts off the trail, Scott thanked Macklin for his support, but added that he was quite capable of fighting his own battles.

'That may well be, but I don't want an important witness getting hurt or killed before I find out what you knew. Jarrett is a dangerous man and there are claims that he is pretty quick on the trigger. It's my guess that your troubles with him might only just be starting. Cowell should have stepped in there, but he didn't. That sergeant will probably get into trouble later for doing what the officer should have done.'

'I'm not scared of Jarrett. I think he relies a lot on bluff.'

The deputy let his grim face relax into what was almost a smile. 'I agree with you there. Don't give him any chances, though, because if he's forced into a fight, he's sure to fight dirty.'

The landslide was steep with plenty of loose earth and rocks on its surface and as his mule carefully picked its way to the bottom, Scott could only marvel at his luck in avoiding more serious injury. The path made by the dead mule was easy to see and they found it with all four rigid legs in the air in among some pine seedlings. The saddle and bridle were missing.

Brannigan did not dismount, but looked about. He pointed to the tracks of several unshod ponies. 'Whoever took that saddle has ridden all over any of the original foot that might have been left.'

'Do you reckon it was the Indians?' Scott asked.

'Could be. Just think for a bit. Were those injuns painted for war?'

'I don't recall. I got my head down mighty quick.'

'Were they carryin' lances or shields?'

'I can't recall.'

The old man nodded. 'I think what you saw was a

huntin' party that got curious about all the shootin'. I know everyone wants to blame it on the Cheyenne, but at this stage I have my doubts. Let's find the fella you shot. How far away is he?'

Scott confidently led the others to where he had left McComb, but when he arrived he found that the dead man was missing. 'His friends might have collected him but he was right here.'

'I know that,' Macklin said. 'There's bloodstains on a couple of those stones. What do you make of the tracks, Dick?'

'Them injuns Scott saw were here but they might just have been lookin' around. Stay where you are so you don't ride over any signs while I have a look around. There's a few moccasin tracks that are interestin'.'

The old man dismounted and cast about like a hound looking for a scent. He looked at the ground from several angles and a short while later rejoined the others. 'I can tell you this,' he announced triumphantly. 'Them polecats went to a lot of trouble to make it look like there was no carcase layin' around and to make it look like the Cheyenne was involved, but they made one mistake. See them tracks over there? You can see where a fella in moccasins got on his pony. He was a white man.'

'Are you sure of that?' Macklin asked.

Brannigan gave a cackling laugh. 'They can't fool me. Whoever left that track got on from the nearside. Injuns get on their ponies from the offside. That was a white man for sure or maybe someone of mixed race. If you go back and tell the others, I'll follow up a few tracks and join you later.'

'Will you be safe on your own?' Scott asked.

'Don't worry about him,' Macklin said. 'He'll make good and sure he sees trouble before it sees him. Now let's get back to the others.'

After a steep scramble up the hillside the pair caught up with the rest of the party. Cowell listened to the information they gave but did not seem unduly worried. Jarrett made no comment, but the sour expression on his face showed that he had no intention of forgetting the recent confrontation with Scott and Macklin. Ruskin said little and stayed well in the background as though fearful of Jarrett.

The trail levelled out as they reached the crest of the range and on a high rocky rise, they saw a roughly constructed blockhouse with a flat roof, a mast for signal flags and a corral nearby.

A soldier standing at a railed section of the roof beside a heliograph waved as he saw the party approaching.

'Here we are,' the sergeant announced. 'Welcome to Signal Station Number Three.'

FIVE

A tall lieutenant with a drooping, sandy moustache emerged from the blockhouse as the party halted. He introduced himself as Leonard Wells, in command of the three signal stations. After telling the newcomers to make themselves comfortable, he called aside his sergeant; Cowell and Macklin went into the building to compare notes. An army cook started preparing coffee for the party and placed a box of hardtack on a stump that served duty as a table. After the long ride even that rough fare was welcome.

Jarrett, Ruskin and Cowell's two men pointedly ignored Scott and retired to the shady side of the blockhouse, leaving him to take care of the mules. Given the attitude of the others, that arrangement suited him just fine.

A couple of soldiers came over and started a conversation in an attempt to relieve the monotony of their situation. They talked for a while about the day's happenings and one man mentioned the fire that their sentry had seen the previous night. He said it was too big to have been an Indian fire and had burned for several hours. They were still speculating about a possible connection with the ambush when the officers emerged from their conference.

Cowell walked across to where Scott was waiting. 'There's a flat grassy area and a spring along the range between here and Post Number Two,' he said. 'I want you to take the mules and horses down there to graze and get a drink. It's not far, just follow the ridgeline along and it will be on your left. Wait there and I will have a man sent when we are ready to start back. We are returning to Crossville so it will be a long day.'

Scott had no trouble herding the mules and horses along the crest until he found the area mentioned. There he halted them and allowed the animals to drink and graze. He was strongly tempted to put his riding mule on a long lariat and stretch out for a nap, for the combination of little sleep and considerable exertion was starting to catch up with him. The knowledge that the killers might still be in the area, however, convinced him that staying awake was safer. He rested in the shade, but when he felt drowsiness coming on, he would pick up his carbine and walk around for a while.

He was standing looking out over the distant reservation when he heard two quick gunshots from the pine forest immediately below where he was standing. There was a crashing in the timber and the sound of a horse galloping over rocks and Brannigan, Dragoon Colt in hand, burst out of the timber.

'Watch out, sonny,' the old man called.

Scott cocked his carbine and crouched behind a convenient rock as he sought the source of danger. Apart from Brannigan and his mount, he saw no other movement.

The old man brought his sweaty roan pony to a halt beside him and slipped from the saddle. 'Someone was just about to bushwhack you,' he panted. 'Saw him just in time. Get them critters rounded up – I'll cover you.'

'Did you get him?'

'No, get movin'.'

The shots had disturbed the stock and Scott had no trouble rounding them up on his mule and pointing them back towards the signal post. When they were trotting in the desired direction, Brannigan mounted his pony and followed.

The men at the post had been alerted and were waiting with rifles at the ready when the other two arrived.

'What was that shooting?' demanded Lieutenant Wells.

'It was me,' Brannigan admitted. 'I was comin' up the mountain and saw someone drawin' a bead on young Bailey. I took a couple of quick shots, but I don't think I hit him. Didn't see anyone else, but he got away.'

41

'Was it a white man or an Indian?'

'I'm not sure. All I could see was a red shirt and big floppy black hat and a rifle lining up Scott. Some injuns wear hats too. There was just time for two pistol shots before he disappeared into the brush. I figger he was gonna kill him and run off the stock.'

'Sounds like an Indian trick to me,' Cowell observed.

Macklin disagreed. 'There's plenty of white men would do that too. Around here we have moonshiners, whiskey peddlers, gun runners, horse and cattle thieves and about every kind of low-life known to man. It would not be hard to buy the services of some of these.'

Wells turned to his sergeant. 'Send a heliograph to Post Two to be relayed to Fort Harris. We need a cavalry troop up here to have a good look around.'

Scott walked over to where Brannigan was reloading his big revolver. 'Thanks for saving my life, Dick. I had no idea anyone was about.'

'That happens in big timber country,' the old man said dismissively, as he poured black powder from a small flask into the revolver's chamber.

Scott watched the loading procedure with interest. 'I didn't think anyone would still be messing about with loose powder and bullets and caps these days.'

Brannigan inserted a lead ball and rammed it home with the loading lever before replying, 'I don't use this gun for people-shootin', don't do much of that these days, but it was the handiest gun I had when I saw that polecat was linin' you up. These old Colts are just dandy for runnin' buffalo injun-style. They might be a mite old-fashioned, but each chamber holds a lot more powder than the forty grains that they are supposed to take and the Dragoon Colt won't blow up like the Walker did. With extra big loads in the chambers, it is still the most powerful pistol around. It's easy as powerful as some carbines and shoots straight if it's pointed straight. With my injun buffalo pony and this old gun I can get any buffalo I go after. That fella who nearly got you was a good seventy yards away, but I gave him the fright of his miserable life.'

'I'm mighty glad you did,' Scott said with conviction. 'Did you see anything in your travels?'

'There're about half a dozen of 'em, whites or maybe a 'breed or two. I followed 'em up to where there was a big fire last night, but there was only trash there, bits of old blankets and boxes and stuff like that. I figgered I was a bit too close to 'em and was headin' back for help when I ran into you. I'm damned if I know what that fire was all about. At first I thought they was burnin' that feller you killed, but there weren't no trace of a body. There's more to this than just an ambush and robbery. I ain't quite figgered it out, but somethin' don't sit right to my way of thinkin'.'

Macklin announced that he had enough information to start preliminary investigations and would return to Crossville until he could compare notes at a later date with the cavalry patrol. That arrangement suited Cowell and he gave orders that his party should also prepare for the return trip.

Jarrett strolled across to where Scott was holding his saddled mule. He asked abruptly, 'Did you see that man Brannigan shot at?'

'No – why's that?'

'Because there might not have been anyone there. When some of these old mountain men are being paid by the day, a lot will try to keep things going as long as they can. I don't know why the sheriff insists on sending that old goat out in cases like this.'

Scott disagreed. 'From what I saw of him, Brannigan knows his business. He read the tracks below the landslide well enough to know that the ones who ambushed us were probably white men.'

Jarrett scoffed. 'He's always been a bit soft on the Indians. That old skunk will say anything he thinks folks will believe. Don't trust him an inch.'

Suspecting that the mule packer had some reason for his sudden questioning, Scott was immediately on his guard. He refrained from making any further comment about Brannigan's activities and resolved to ask a few people about Jarrett when he finally learned on whom he could rely. Being a stranger in the district had put him at considerable disadvantage.

At one stage when the others were out of earshot, he asked Ruskin, 'What to you think of all of this?'

The packer looked around nervously before replying, 'I ain't paid to think, and mind my own business.

It's smartest not to know too much about what's going on sometimes.'

'Why's that?'

'That's all I'm saying. If you're smart you won't ask questions. Just do your job and see only what you're supposed to see.'

Having delivered that advice, the packer moved away quickly as though he feared being seen talking to Scott.

They took their leave of the troops at the signal station and turned their mounts back towards Crossville. Glancing back over his shoulder Scott saw two soldiers on the blockhouse roof adjusting the mirrors on the heliograph before flashing a message to the next post.

The ride would be a long one and would finish in the dark, but the packers expected little rest on the following day as they were bringing home Newton's body for burial. Jarrett predicted that for a while too, they would be kept busy training more mules from the government herd kept at the depot.

Once past the landslide, the trail was easier and the party's leaders were clustered ahead of the others, talking and smoking as they went. Scott was riding beside Brannigan and noticed that the old man's face was pale and that he seemed short of breath.

'You don't look too good, Dick. How are you feeling?'

The reply came slowly and softly and belied the

speaker's appearance. 'I'm fine – just gettin' too old for all this stuff. Don't feel like it now – but after a rest – gonna' try to figger out – why them bush-whackers started that fire. Reckon they was tryin' to hide somethin'. That soldier fella, Cowell, ain't exactly bustin' a gut to find out what happened. There's more to this deal than folks think.'

'You could be right about that. Macklin seems genuine enough, but Cowell and Jarrett ain't exactly keen to find out what happened. I get the impression they want to write this whole thing off as an Indian raid.'

'You ain't as dumb as I thought,' Brannigan whispered. He coughed and when he regained his breath, he said, 'Watch Jarrett. He's a bad one.'

'You don't sound too good. Do you want to stop?'

'Can't talk much, keep goin'. Be right when I get home to bed.'

Curious, though reluctant to press the old man further, Scott rode beside him for the rest of the journey, but refrained from speaking.

The lights of Crossville were in view when a red glow lit up the night sky. 'There's a fire in town,' Macklin called. 'Looks like it's a big one.'

As all eyes turned towards the distant blaze, Brannigan suddenly grunted, gasped and fell from his horse.

SIX

Macklin also saw the old man fall and dismounted at the same time as Scott. The deputy knelt beside Brannigan, briefly tried to revive him, but then shook his head. 'It's no use,' he told the others. 'I reckon poor old Dick was dead before he hit the ground.'

'We can't help him now,' Cowell said. 'I'm taking my men on ahead. That fire could wipe out half the town. We can't be slowed down by two dead men. Already we have two riders on one horse.'

The deputy had the solution to the problem. 'We can leave the bodies here with someone to keep the coyotes away and send a wagon out for them in the morning.'

The lieutenant wasted few words. 'Bailey – get those two bodies over there under the trees and wait for a wagon in the morning. Let's get going before all of Crossville burns.'

Scott saw little point in objecting. He was nearing

47

exhaustion and the bruises of the previous day were feeling sore. It would be a hungry, uncomfortable night, but with any luck he could enjoy a rest.

The deputy helped him move the two corpses to an easily accessible place and quickly remounted his horse. The others were already moving when he turned his mount and spurred after them.

Scott quickly unsaddled his mule and Brannigan's pony, tethering both on lariats so they were able to graze and set about building a fire. On a sudden inspiration, he rummaged around in Brannigan's crudely made saddle-bags and found a few strips of hard, dried, jerked beef. At least there would be something to eat.

With food, fire and a makeshift bed of saddle blankets, he settled down in reasonable comfort for the night. Mindful of his previous encounters, he set up his bed away from the fire where he would not be easily seen by unwelcome night visitors. He also kept the carbine loaded and close at hand.

A couple of times through the night he was awakened by the snorting of the pony or the mule, but was reassured to see them lower their heads and start grazing again. They would not do that if something had aroused their suspicions.

Suddenly the stars were gone, the sky had paled and it was morning. Scott sat up with a start and was reassured to see the animals dozing on their tethers. As he pushed aside the blanket, he realized just how parched he felt. His last drink had been at the signal station, the afternoon before. From his first trip through the area, he knew that the trail was roughly parallel to the creek, so buckling on his revolver and picking up his carbine and ammunition belt, he started into the trees. A short walk found him at the sloping bank of a shallow stream. Stretching full length on the ground, he sucked up the cold water, paused a while and drank again. It was so cold and refreshing that he was about to have a bit more water when he heard a sound in the brush, as though a heavy animal was forcing its way through the close-growing vegetation. Then he heard another sound and was sure he was hearing two horses. Seconds later, he glimpsed two riders in single file about fifty yards away as they made their way through the foliage.

Both men were leaning forward as they rode, like hunters expecting to see game, giving Scott the distinct feeling that he was their quarry.

Neither man was remarkable in appearance, just bearded, rough-looking types in well-worn clothes. If there was anything distinctive it was the heavy armaments they carried. Each appeared to have a pair of revolvers, a large knife on his belt and a rifle in one hand. The nearest one had long, straggling, sandy hair and a beard to match. He looked slightly younger than his companion, who was black-bearded and dark enough to be part Mexican or Indian.

Scott's first impulse was to hide but he knew these men would not go away. Reluctantly he decided to

49

confront them, but at a time and place that best
suited him. Quietly he loaded the carbine and began
stalking the pair.

The morning dew had softened the grass and
foliage and he found that he could move almost
silently. Slipping quietly from one sheltering patch of
brush or tree trunk to the next, he was able to keep
the pair in sight and to close the gap between them.
They halted at the edge of the timber overlooking
the clearing where he had been camped. The pair
leaned together, whispering and pointing as though
planning an ambush.

The sandy one was carrying a Winchester repeater
while his companion had a single-shot Sharps. Given
that his own rifle was a single-shot, Scott knew that
the man with the repeater represented the most
danger. Sighting on him he called, 'Hands up – don't
move!'

The pair obeyed neither command, and with
unexpected speed wheeled their horses around. The
man with the Winchester raised his rifle as he turned,
the butt already pulled into his shoulder and the fore-
stock resting across his raised bridle arm.

Scott squeezed the trigger without hesitation.
Through a cloud of powder smoke, he saw the man
fall from his horse. He felt the draught of something
and heard the boom of the dark one's rifle. The man
had missed but not by much, his accuracy affected by
shooting from a moving horse.

Both men, their rifles empty, discarded them.

Reloading under such circumstances would not be possible. The dark man went for the six-shooter at his side, but Scott took a chance and ran to where the fallen man's Winchester lay. Luck was with him because the loose horse momentarily screened him from the gunman. He snatched up the rifle and fired at his opponent.

His first shot missed and the dark-haired rider fired back. His shot also went wide of the mark. Steadying himself, Scott worked the loading lever, took deliberate aim and fired again. This time his bullet struck home. The man doubled up momentarily, but managed to stay on his horse. Aware of the disadvantage he was facing, he wheeled his mount and slumped in the saddle and spurred away.

Any attempt to shoot the fleeing man was forgotten as he heard a shot behind him. The bullet, fired by a failing hand, went nowhere near him. He spun about to see the sandy-haired man struggling to cock his revolver for another shot.

'Don't do it. I don't want to shoot you again.'

'You won't need to. I'm gone, but I'm taking you with me – you sonofabitch.'

Even as he struggled with his final threat, though, the man on the ground suddenly weakened and the gun fell from his hand as the light faded from his eyes.

Scott approached cautiously until he was sure that the man was dead. Then he gathered up the fallen weapons and caught his late opponent's horse that was standing nearby, ground hitched by the fallen reins.

He examined the horse and saw at once that it was a very good breed. It's bright bay coat and legs were spattered with mud and pushing through the brush had tangled its mane and tail but the quality of the animal was obvious.

'I wonder where he stole you from,' Scott said as he stroked the animal's head. A glance at the brand on the shoulder supplied no answer. It was indistinct and after several tries he found that he still was not sure what it was. 'You're wearing a real rustler's brand, but you look like a good, honest horse to me.'

He could not relax because he was not sure how disabled the escaped rider was. If only slightly wounded the man might return and, worse still, might bring along some of his friends. Tethering the horse, he selected a good defensive spot among some boulders and fallen timber and carried the captured weapons there. Then he settled down to wait.

He calculated that approximately an hour had dragged by before he heard the rattle of a wagon on the road coming from the direction of Crossville. When it came into view Scott saw a big man of uncertain age in a dusty black coat hunched in the driver's seat.

'Howdy,' he said as he reined in the two-horse team. 'I'm George Basser, the local undertaker. Sheriff Hennessey says there's two dead men to collect.'

'Well, actually there are three now.'

'Hennessey reckoned there were only two.'

'There's three now and I reckon the sheriff will be mighty happy to see your latest customer. I suggest we get them loaded because this one might have friends who won't appreciate him getting shot.'

The latter remark spurred Basser into action and they set to work loading their grim cargo on to the wagon. Scott also threw in the saddles from both horses along with the weapons he had collected. He decided to ride the dead man's horse and swapped to his own saddle, but attached the Winchester in its scabbard in case of trouble. The pony and mule would be herded loose beside the wagon.

'What happened about that fire we saw last night?'

Basser frowned before replying, 'All hell busted loose last night. The army stores depot got burned to the ground and a soldier is missing. He might have set the fire and deserted or he might be dead in the ruins. No one knows at this stage.'

SEVEN

The stores depot was just a smoking pile of ashes mixed with odd pieces of heat-twisted metal when Scott and Basser reached town. People were standing about discussing the night's events and more than one complained about the stench emanating from the ruins. Some who had never seen burnt buildings before could only compare it to the smell of rotting garbage, but the odour was all too familiar to those on the frontier who had experienced fires.

Hennessey, his clothes and face still smoke-blackened from a night of firefighting, was standing in front of his office when the undertaker halted the wagon in front of him. The news that he had another corpse to deal with did nothing for his frayed temper.

'I reckon you have some explaining to do, Bailey. This place was nice and quiet until you came along. Put those loose animals in the government mule corral and get back quick. I'll fix things with Gilmore about their feed. I want you back here damned quick. I need my sleep.'

Scott drove the pony and mule down the street towards the depot and, on the way, passed Mary Hegarty driving a buckboard. As both were fully occupied, they each gave a brief wave and went on.

Gilmore was at the corral when Scott arrived. He scowled as he was told the latest news and grudgingly ordered Scott to return to the sheriff's office and arranged to see him after that.

Cantering back up the street, he dismounted at the office and hitched the horse to the rail outside. Macklin, bleary-eyed after a couple of hours' rest in an empty cell, was waiting with his boss. The weapons and personal effects of Brannigan and the dead gunman were in two separate piles on a long bench beside one wall.

The lawmen wasted no time in getting down to business. Scott, with no reason to hold anything back, gave a truthful version of the morning's events, but did not know if his questioners really believed him.

Hennessey did most of the talking while Macklin jotted down certain notes with a pencil and paper.

Finally the sheriff seemed satisfied. 'You will need to be a witness at the coroner's inquiry,' he said, 'so stay around Crossville for a while.'

'Suits me. Do you now the name of the *hombre* I shot?'

'He was a bad character named Carson Wood. He had a prison record and we suspected him of a lot of crimes, but could never get enough evidence to arrest him. He used to come and go, but never seemed to have a fixed address or a regular job.'

'I have his horse outside. Is there any chance that I could buy it?'

Hennessey had more worries than a dead man's horse. 'I don't know. It could be stolen. If you want to look after it and keep it fed and exercised, that's fine by me. If no one claims it after all the dust has settled, we can probably do some sort of deal about it. I'll fix things up with Rafe Gilmore so you can keep it at the government mule corrals if you are prepared to pay for its feed.'

'Sounds like a good deal to me, sheriff. You know where to find me when you need me.' Scott hoped he had sufficiently concealed his elation and was anxious to get the horse away before the lawman had second thoughts.

He mounted the horse and had barely ridden a hundred yards when he encountered Mary Hegarty coming in the opposite direction in her buckboard.

She halted the team as they drew level, glanced at his mount and said, 'Scott, where did you get that horse? I always had an idea of buying that one for myself.'

'I'm looking after him temporarily. Sounds like you know something about him.'

'I've seen him before a few times. His rider was a rough-looking character and I heard he could be a dangerous man so I didn't like to approach him. He used to hang around the mule corrals when he was in town, but he never stayed for long. There were always antisocial types hanging around those corrals.'

'Men who pack mules tend to be rough-looking. Mules ain't fussy if you haven't shaved or forget to wear a clean shirt.'

'It's more than that. Some of these characters are loaded down with guns and knives. I notice Sheriff Hennessey seems to keep an eye on them too. That horse's owner had a friend, another bad-looking *hombre* who used to ride a buckskin horse. It wasn't bad, but not as good as that bay.'

The gunman Scott had wounded was riding a buckskin horse so he asked, 'So you think someone at the mule corral would know this horse, and maybe who rode it and maybe even the buckskin's rider?'

Mary laughed. 'They're sure to. He looks a little rough now but he is still an eye-catching sort. Those packers aren't blind. Someone there could probably tell you more about him.'

'Will you be in town for long? I could let you know what I find out.' Scott was prepared to use any excuse to see more of this girl.

Mary shook her head. 'I'm afraid not. This is just a quick trip to get some stores that my mother accidentally left off her monthly store order. However, our ranch is only six miles out on the Hidden Creek road. If you ever take that horse for a ride you could call in and see us. I have to go now so that I am home before dark. Don't forget. Call in if you're out our way.'

'I'll do that,' Scott promised as both resumed their separate journeys.

He was unsaddling at the mule corral when Jarrett appeared with an angry scowl on his face.

'What's that horse doing here? This is government property.'

Scott was fast becoming sick of the packer's continual bad moods, but kept his anger in check. 'I'm looking after it until there's a coroner's report on its owner. The sheriff is fixing things with Gilmore. Do you know anything about this horse?'

'Why the hell should I?'

'I heard its rider used to come down here sometimes. He had a friend who rode a buckskin horse.'

'Whoever told you that is a damn liar or it happened some time when I was out with the pack train. Who was it?'

Scott had the feeling that Jarrett was lying and could not resist the urge to worry him a bit more. 'I can't tell you,' he replied. 'The one concerned might be called later as a witness.'

The packer looked hard at him. 'A witness to what?'

Satisfied with the note of anxiety in Jarrett's voice, Scott casually told him, 'Hell, I don't know. That's for the law to decide. I ain't a lawyer.'

Next morning a stranger stepped off the coach that plied between the railroad and Crossville. He was short and broad, somewhere in his early forties with fair hair and a small moustache. His face seemed frozen in a disapproving look and his blue eyes were cold and unfriendly. The brown suit was crumpled and dusty from the coach journey and a bulge on his left hip advertised that he was carrying a gun. His derby hat, fashionable in the city, but impractical for the frontier, was set low on his forehead as if to partially conceal his frown.

Cedric Maley did not like small western towns and saw no reason for concealing that dislike, or for that matter, any other of his many dislikes. The sooner his work in Crossville was done, the happier he would be.

He booked in at the hotel and strolled out into the street. The blackened ruins of the stores depot were visible from where he stood and he saw no point in going there. Instead he saw the sheriff's office on the other side of the road so made his enquiries there.

Macklin was on duty and after a brief discussion, directed him to the mule corrals where Lieutenant Cowell had set up temporary operations in a shed loaned to him by Gilmore.

The soldier was writing, his work supported by a packing case that had been brought into service as a desk, and looked up in surprise as the stranger entered.

'I take it you are Lieutenant Cowell. My name is Maley.' The newcomer reached into a coat pocket and produced a rather well-worn brown envelope. He tossed it on the desk. 'This letter will tell you why

I'm here. I think you would have been expecting me.'

The officer opened the letter and read it quickly. The letterhead was impressive and the instructions were clear. He was to render Maley every assistance. He forced a smile but it made no impression on the grim person standing before him. 'How may I help you?'

'You can start by telling me all you know about the recent pack-train ambush and finish by telling me what you know about how the army stores depot came to be destroyed. And don't leave out too much of what happened between those two events.'

The lieutenant indicated an empty box that now served as a chair. 'Take a seat, Mr Maley. I'll help all I can. From where exactly do you want me to start?'

'You can start when that new man, Bailey, came on to the scene.'

Cowell was surprised that Maley knew about Scott, but did not betray his unease. 'Rafe Gilmore hired him. He was looking for work, seemed to have rea-sonable knowledge of mule packing. Gilmore is the civilian contractor who runs the pack train. I didn't see Bailey until the following morning when he went out with Ed Newton with supplies for the army signal stations in the Big Pine mountains. He didn't impress me much, but I reckoned that Gilmore knew what he was doing.'

'What exactly did you dislike about Bailey?'

'He was a drifter who might have had a shady past.

There was something about him that aroused my suspicions but it is hard to say exactly what. I am not sure that I believe his stories about the original ambush and some things that happened later. Much of it does not ring true.'

'Such as?'

'That first attack was almost certainly the work of Indians from the nearby reservation. Bailey claimed there were white men involved. He said he killed one but the body never came to light. He killed another man a couple of days ago but Sheriff Hennessey knows more about that than I do. He might trust him but I don't. One of the packers is a bit suspicious of him too.'

'Who is that?'

'Lije Garrett is Gilmore's best packer and a good judge of men. He told me he suspects that Scott Bailey is hiding something.'

'I'll interview Jarrett later but first, what was the pack train carrying?'

'The usual stuff: food, ammunition, blankets and a few of those buffalo coats for winter use by the signallers. I can't give accurate details because all our records were destroyed in the fire.'

'But there were more than records destroyed,' prompted Maley.

'That's right. The remains of private Arthur Meade were found in the ashes. As far as we could ascertain, Meade must have been sleeping off a session on the booze when the fire caught him. He might have even caused it by dropping a cigarette or something like that.'

'It sounds like Private Meade was a little too fond of alcohol.'

'You could say that.'

Maley fixed him with a hard glare and then continued. 'I know you would only have an approximate idea, but what do you think was the value of the supplies stolen?'

Cowell thought for a few moments. 'It could be as much as two thousand dollars. Those buffalo coats are worth thirty dollars apiece and there were a few of them. Then there was food, blankets, ammunition, tobacco and other small items. Thirteen mules are missing too; top-quality government mules are worth more than most cow ponies around here.'

They talked for more than an hour and Cowell gradually began to feel a little more confident in his replies. He formed the impression that Maley was pretending to have more information than he actually had. Despite his all-knowing air, the inquisitor seemed to be fishing for clues and in the process was inclined to accept vague answers in some cases.

Finally Maley rose a little stiffly from his seat. 'Thank you, Mr Cowell. I might have a few more details to get from you later. but first I'll have a word with Scott Bailey.'

EIGHT

Scott was greasing some pack harness when he saw the grim-faced stranger hurrying towards him .The harness-draped corral fence was between them and the shorter man peered through between the top and second rails.

'Are you Scott Bailey?'

'That's right. What can I do for you?'

'My name is Cedric Maley. I've been sent by the War Department to investigate what's been going on around here. I need to ask you a few questions and I want straight answers.'

'You go ahead and ask your questions and if they are straight questions you'll get straight answers. But if you start playing with words or trying to trap me somehow, you can go to hell. Now ask your doggone questions.'

Maley looked slightly affronted that Bailey was not in awe of him, but started his questioning. The queries were brief and blunt as though there was an urgency to the case that was not apparent to Scott. Having nothing to hide, the latter had no difficulty in supplying answers, but as the process continued he started to realize just how little he knew about that first fateful trip.

Maley's eyes narrowed suspiciously as Scott described his experience of that day. 'You say that the train was already packed when you arrived for work. Don't you think it was a little odd seeing as you were there to learn the business?'

'I did and I thought at first that I had the starting time wrong, but then Jarrett told me they had started early because Ed Newton had been on the whiskey the night before and wanted to get on the road before he was too sick to start. I guess Jarrett and a couple of Cowell's men helped him pack.'

'Do you know what the train was carrying?'

'No. I asked Ed, but he was pretty vague about it and mumbled something about it being the usual supplies.'

The interrogation continued and Maley showed considerable interest when told of the ambush, the shooting of McComb and subsequent happenings at the signal station. He was obviously disappointed when he found that only Brannigan had followed up Scott's version of events but had been unable to verify his findings. 'So Brannigan never had time to make a complete report even though he claimed to have saved you from being shot?'

'That's right. He might have said more to Tom

Macklin, but he only told me that there were white men involved and not just Indians as Cowell and Jarrett seemed to think.'

'And the lookouts at the signal station saw nothing?'

'One of them said he saw a fire through the night, but the tall trees stopped them seeing much in daylight. It might have been Indian hunters camped outside the reservation or it might have been McComb's friends but I am only guessing. Nobody seemed to think it was important.'

'Probably not – anything else?'

'One more thing – those two characters I tangled with the other day knew where I was. I think someone from town might have sent them.'

'Why would they do that? 'Maley demanded sharply.

'I've thought about it a lot and think it might have been McComb's friends looking for revenge. They could have been sent by someone in the town here. I can't think of any other reason.'

'You didn't have any information you were keeping to yourself by any chance?'

Scott shook his head. 'Nobody told me much at all. I was kept well and truly in the dark.'

Maley turned to leave. 'Thanks for the information, Bailey. I have to see the sheriff and will probably get back to you again soon. I must ask you to stay around town for the next couple of days.'

Scott was far from happy as he was looking forward

to a ride out to the Hegarty place on the weekend. He could only hope that Maley would have finished his inquiries by them.

Another day passed. As the pack train had stopped running, Scott was put to work breaking a couple of new mules to both saddle and pack. It was work that he liked, but there was a disturbing air of uncertainty and much speculation about rejoining the rest of the train at Fort Harris. He had just taken the first ride on a mule when he noticed Corporal Wade watching him. He had found Wade to be one of the more friendly characters with whom he was working.

'Looks like I was wasting my time,' the soldier joked. 'I thought that jackass would buck. Things are mighty quiet around here since the fire. I was counting on you for a bit of entertainment.'

'Have you any idea what's going to happen to us?'

'I'm not sure what's going on. We have been told to wait here while the sheriff and Hangman Maley are trying to piece things together.'

'I hadn't heard Maley called Hangman before. Sounds like he ain't the most popular *hombre* around. Where does he fit into things?'

'He's attached to the Quartermaster's Department and investigates irregularities with army stores and equipment. He always tacks the blame on to someone and if stories are right, it don't matter if they are innocent. If he can build a case against them, they are guilty. Be very careful what you say to him because he's likely to twist your words and use

them against you. He has been interviewing us soldiers and I reckon you packers will be next. We told
him nothing he could use and if you're smart you'll
do the same.'

'Thanks for the advice,' Scott said as he unsaddled
the mule. 'I'll be careful.'

Later that day Maley came around to the corrals
where Scott was working. His face was still set in his
usual expression of disapproval that contradicted the
friendly tone he adopted. His visit was completely different from the searching interview the packer was
expecting. 'I need your help, Bailey. How would you
like to take a nice ride out in the mountains?'

Scott's reply was guarded. 'That all depends. My
last rides out in the mountains could hardly be
described as nice ones. What's on your mind?'

'I'm interested in some of the things that happened on your first day with Gilmore's outfit. I'm
told you are a former cowhand and assume that like
most of your calling, you know the rudiments of
tracking. Do you?'

'Most cattlemen learn to track strayed stock to
some degree, but that don't make me an expert. If
you expect me to say that such-and-such a horse was
carrying a left-handed rider or something of that
kind, you can forget it. Under the right conditions, I
might be able to track the horse but not much else.'

'That might be enough. A lot of folks around here
doubt your version of things that have happened and
I'm giving you a chance to prove what you have

claimed. There are others who think you know more than you are saying and still others who think you might even be in cahoots with those killers. As an outsider, you are a prime target for suspicion. This is your chance to shut down some of the silly stories that are flying around about you.'

'I'll damn soon shut them down if they say those things to my face.' Scott was still unsure whether Maley was speaking the truth or was trying a divide-and-conquer approach with the packers.

'I would like to take a ride out and see the scene of the ambush where Newton was killed. Then I would like to see if the attackers left any tracks we could follow. I am not sure that the late Mr Brannigan followed them far enough. You would be able to point out where things happened and would be reasonably familiar with parts of that country now. Would you be prepared to come with me?'

'I'll go if you can square things with Gilmore. I want to hold on to this job for a while yet.'

'I can fix things with Gilmore. He can be trusted, but I'm not too sure of anyone else.'

'That makes two of us because I know that those two characters who came after me came from town. Someone knew exactly where I was and sent that pair out. But I can't figure out why.'

'It could be revenge. They might have been friends of Mc Comb. That's all I can figure. Unless—' Maley paused theatrically as though thinking hard and continued: 'It could be that they want to shut you up. My guess is that Brannigan might have told you something important before he died, or some people think he might have. This isn't just an ordinary ambush by Indians or bandits. Certain people are gunning for you and I think you will be safer out in the mountains with me than you will be around Crossville.'

'I'd like to think so, but I am not sure. You didn't exactly come highly recommended.'

'You can form your own opinions about me on the trail. I have borrowed a horse from Sheriff Hennessey and a carbine and ammunition from Lieutenant Cowell. We'll be travelling light, just a blanket and poncho apiece, and I'll be picking up a bit of food from McRae's store. It won't be much, but will have to do. We start in the morning before daylight.'

'Suits me, but it seems that half the town is going to know we ain't around and it won't take a real smart fella to figure out where we're likely to be.'

'That's what I'm counting on. We have to bring these characters out into the open.'

'I am starting to feel that I could be the bait in some sort of trap.'

'That's very perceptive of you, Bailey, because you are.'

NINE

Scott turned in his saddle and looked at the rider following. He bore little resemblance to the Maley he
had first seen. The derby hat was gone, replaced by a
misshapen wide-brimmed arrangement that looked
as though it had been packed in the bottom of the
investigator's luggage. The collar and tie had been
replaced by a bandanna and the coat strapped
behind the saddle was a much more substantial one
that the suit coat worn around town. Maley's short -
barrelled Merwin & Hulbert .44 now hung from a
full cartridge belt and its owner looked quite at
home on the horse he bestrode. I had you wrong,
Scott told himself, those town clothes fooled me.
This character is no chair-bound clerk from a
Washington office.

They had left town early hoping that they would
attract little attention, but Corporal Wade was
already astir when they left the mule corrals. The
soldier was trying to coax a fire from the ashes of the

campfire that had served as a rough kitchen for Cowell and his men. He waved to Bailey and continued fanning the smouldering coals with his hat.

It was full daylight when they reached the place where Bailey had fought the two gunmen. The tracks had been trampled over and there was little to gain from them so they did not delay for long.

Had it not been for a sense of unknown, lurking danger, Scott would have enjoyed the ride that alternated between cool, shady forest and sunny patches that the early sun was just reaching. It was an ideal time for hunting and being so close to the Cheyenne reservation there could be Indian hunting parties in the area. Though a peace of sorts existed some of the young bucks were unlikely to resist the urge to take two easy scalps if temptation came their way.

They rode to the foot of the landslide and viewed what the scavengers had left of Scott's mule. Many horse tracks still showed, some made by unshod ponies and others by shod horses.

'Saw four Indians near here just after I shot McComb,' Scott said. 'I can't say, though, that they were part of the gang. They could have been a hunting party attracted by the shots.'

'I'll be just as happy if we don't meet them. Keep a sharp eye out, Bailey.'

The trail led around the base of the mountains and at one point it was intersected by a mass of tracks descending from the trail above. The smaller, narrower prints of mule hoofs were plainly visible on soft patches and bare earth.

Scott pointed. 'This is where the killers drove the mules after they ambushed the train. I reckon Brannigan would have followed these, but I don't know how far he went. He might have been diverted by the tracks of the man who went up the range to shoot me.'

'Let's follow the mule tracks and move on. I doubt we'll learn much from the main trail.' Maley was urging his mount forward impatiently even as he spoke.

It was near noon when they came to a stretch of open country. It was about a hundred yards across and in the centre was a blackened area where a large fire had been burning.

'I think we'll find where those killers disposed of your late friend, McComb,' Maley said confidently, but he was wrong.

They found no human remains and very little else except pieces of charred wooden boxes, burnt scraps of sacking, odd pieces of charred leather harness and what looked like the remains of a few blankets.

They dismounted and looked around. Both were puzzled and made no attempt to hide the fact.

'It looks to me like they unloaded the packs here and repacked the mules,' Scott said. 'They must have been sure nobody was following them. But why would they do that?'

Maley walked about frowning and occasionally kicking at charred debris. 'I was told that one of the

army signal posts reported a fire down here somewhere the night after the ambush. This must have
been what they saw. But it makes no sense. Why
would they repack the loads?'

'Damned if I know,' Scott replied. 'But let's get
after those mules. I don't like standing out here in
the open. Someone could be watching us from one
of the high places around here.'

'Getting nervous, Bailey?'

'You're damned right I am.'

For once Maley's hard face almost managed a
smile. 'I'll let you in on a secret – so am I.'

Luther Ashton looked again, then snapped shut the
small brass telescope and climbed down from his
vantage point on the top of a large boulder. He saw
the two riders at the site of the fire and knew that he
must warn his companions. Given that the strangers
were about a mile away, he reckoned he had at least
fifteen minutes before they were close enough to
detect the camp. Once on the ground, he set off at a
run through the thickly growing brush and patches
of lofty pines that screened the hideout.

Mose Dodge was sitting beside the wounded man
who was stretched on a blanket in the shade. He
looked up in alarm as he saw his young associate
racing through the trees.

'Strangers comin' – two of them,' Luther gasped.

Dodge looked at the unconscious man on the
ground. He had taken a bullet in the lung and for

73

the last couple of days his condition had been deteriorating. Moving him was out of the question.

'What do we do?' Ashton followed well, but had never shown any initiative.

'We don't take chances. Start packing up. We're getting out of here. Get those horses saddled and pack up anything we need. I'm guessing those strangers are the law. Let's not tangle with them.'

The younger man ran a few paces towards where the horses were hobbled and suddenly stopped. He turned and pointed to the man on the ground. 'What about Bob?'

'We can't take him. He stays here. He's as good as dead anyway and he might even delay them.'

'But he can't fight and might talk if they can bring him around.'

'He won't talk,' Dodge snapped. 'Don't waste time. Get those horses.'

The tracks were easy to follow and both Scott and Maley had the uneasy feeling that they could lead straight into an ambush. Consequently they moved about five yards apart and advanced cautiously, every sense alert for the first indication of trouble. The wall of green ahead could conceal a dozen killers or nobody at all.

Then they heard the shot. It was strangely muffled, but seemed fairly close at hand. Both were confident, though, that it was not aimed at them. Drawing their revolvers and shortening their grips on the reins, they urged their mounts forward at a steady walk. Somewhere ahead they heard horses crashing through the brush and were slightly reassured as the sounds became more distant.

Ahead, through a break in the trees, Scott noticed a grassy clearing. He pointed silently. Maley nodded, indicating that he too could see the open space. Quietly they urged their mounts forward and halted again at the edge of the cleared ground.

The grass had been grazed and in places was torn up with hoof marks from both horses and mules. Opposite them, where the trees started again, they saw the remains of a campfire. They were halfway across the clearing when they saw the man on the ground, half-concealed in a patch of long grass.

He was facing away from them so both knew that he was not lying in ambush and there was an ominous stillness about him as they rode closer. It was then that the riders saw fresh blood pooling on the ground near the man's head.

'Keep an eye open,' Maley ordered as he dismounted and led his nervously snorting horse forward.

It was plain that the man on the ground was dead. Someone had shot him in the head. The reason for this became obvious when the pair noticed the improvised bandage made from a shirt that was fastened around his body. It was stiff with dried blood from an earlier wound.

'Looks like his friends decided not to take him

with them,' Maley said casually with the air of someone familiar with such grisly sights.

Scott forced himself to look more closely. 'I think that's the one I shot the other day. I only got a quick look at him, but I remember he was riding a buckskin horse.'

'I'm going to have a look around here, Bailey. See if you can pick up some tracks and maybe figure out how many men were here and which way they were headed. Be careful though, in case they decide to turn back and ambush you.'

The latter instruction was superfluous because Scott already had the same idea.

He rode around the hoof-torn area. Marks on trees showed where a makeshift rope corral had been used to hold the stolen mules for a while and tracks a few days old showed where they had been driven off into the timber. Further searching revealed fresh tracks made by three horses heading into the dense pine growth of the mountainside.

TEN

'There're fresh tracks of three horses leading up the mountain there – could be two riders and a led horse or three riders,' Scott told Maley. 'Are we going to follow them up?'

The latter looked up from his grim task of searching the dead man's pockets. 'You follow them and see if you can find whether there were three men or only two who escaped. Don't go too far and come back here as soon as you find out how many were here. Be careful they don't lead you into an ambush.'

Again the last instruction was totally unnecessary because the same idea was still foremost in Scott's mind. He followed the tracks for about half a mile. They led upwards towards the crest of the range. Then he found the saddle blanket and on picking it up, he knew that he had the information he sought.

Maley was roaming around the campsite when he returned and announced, 'There were two of them and they were leading that dead *hombre*'s horse.'

The other looked at him and said sharply. 'How do you know? You said yourself that you were no tracker.'

'Don't have to be,' Scott told him, and dropped the saddle blanket at his questioner's feet. 'See the yellow hair on that blanket? I told you that man was riding a buckskin horse when we were swapping lead. Any saddled horse being led without a rider soon loses the saddle blanket, specially in steep country. Our friends didn't wait to pick it up if they noticed it was missing at all.'

If this information impressed Maley, he failed to show it. Instead he pointed to a branding iron leaning against a rope-scarred tree. 'See what you make of that.'

Scott dismounted and examined the iron. It was crudely made in the form of a double B. He showed his companion the heavy-gauge iron that had been forged into the letters. 'Looks like they have rebranded the stolen mules. This iron would be hard to heat up, but you can bet that the thick lines it leaves would help cover any edges of the US brand that it was stamped over. All you need to do now is to notify local lawmen to grab anyone selling mules wearing a fresh BB brand. It was mighty careless of them to leave that iron behind.'

'That makes sense,' Maley admitted, almost as though it was painful for him to do so. 'Now can you take me to one of the signal stations around here?'

'That's easy enough. We just ride to the top of the

range and we're sure to find one of them. But what do we do about that dead man?'

'I'll get the soldiers to send down a detail to bury him. The most important thing is to get out a warning about those mules.'

'Looks like your job will be just about over now,' Scott said hopefully. It was easy to grow tired of Maley's company.

'The mules are only a side issue, Bailey. The real work is only just starting, so you're stuck with me for a while yet.'

Two days later Scott was back at his old job. He was mildly surprised that he was still employed because with no stores to move, he expected that Gilmore's operation would have been ordered to join the main train at Fort Harris. The talk was that some staff would no longer be needed, but Gilmore made no comment when he returned from his ride with Maley. He detected a change in attitude too among the team and at first thought that he might have been accepted. However, he soon found that friendly small-talk from his workmates was interspersed with enough questions to arouse his suspicions. He parried the questions as best he could, saying, quite truthfully, that both Maley and Sheriff Hennessey had told him to say nothing.

Jarrett made a half-hearted attempt to sound friendly, but his old antagonism returned when he learned nothing. Then he tried shock tactics. 'The story is around town that you killed Bob Dawson, wounded him a few days earlier and finished him off when you found him lying wounded later.'

'How would you know?' Scott asked. 'Nobody told me that man's name. Who's been making that claim?'

'It's all over town,' Jarrett said dismissively. 'Seems everyone knows but you.'

'Anyone says that is a liar and anyone who repeats that story is an idiot.'

'Are you calling me an idiot?'

'Either that or you're a liar. You should be smart enough to know which description fits you best. Maybe you're a bit of both.'

The roar of rage and flurry of fists that followed were only to be expected. Under the circumstances most men on the frontier would react the same way. But Scott had been in enough fights to know that the first rush was usually the least dangerous if it was expected. Men would try to end the fight as quickly as possible and little planning or skill went into the initial attack. He took most of the blows on his forearms as he retreated slightly and looked for an opening. It came almost immediately as Jarrett threw caution to the winds and paid for his error. A well-directed left took him full in the mouth, mashing his lips against his teeth. Momentarily the packer stopped and almost stood erect, then came in again with his long arms flailing. A punch came over Scott's guard and lifted a bit of skin from his forehead but he crouched and moved inside that long reach. Even then one looping punch curled around his back and though it did not land cleanly, he felt the power behind it.

A solid left rip into Jarrett's ribs seemed to do him little damage, but might have weakened the blow that Scott took on the shoulder. The packer was a fit man and tough with it. He was prepared to take a few punches to deliver a decisive blow.

Both men scored with punches as they momentarily broke apart and then Jarrett came boring in again as though he had taken the best his opponent could dish out. Scott knew he had landed a few good blows, but it was disheartening to see that they seemed to have had so little effect.

As they came together again, Jarrett grabbed Scott's bandanna in an attempt to pull him into a head butt. But with one hand full and only one to guard his head, it left his opponent the opportunity to launch a two-handed attack. He lost his grip and reeled back under a barrage of short hooks and jabs.

The scuffle attracted the attention of the others at the mule corral and the pair were soon surrounded by a small crowd of spectators. Toe to toe, they traded punches and for a while there was little between them. Scott fought defensively as he found that his opponent was constantly running on to his left hand and if the punches were not as powerful as others, they were doing damage.

Jarrett was bleeding from the mouth and nose,

snorting blood as he closed in again, but was still dangerous and when his blows landed, they hurt. One hook to the side of the head set Scott's ears ringing but luckily he moved back before the packer could follow it up. Then he saw what he was looking for. His opponent had adopted a more upright stance and as he closed in to attack was almost leaning back. It was the stance of a man who had run into too many straight lefts but more damaging was the fact that it stopped him getting the whole weight of his body behind his punches. The odd blows were still landing but some of the sting was gone from them. For all his fitness, Jarrett had not been able to keep up the pace of his earlier attacks. He tried head butts in clinches and used knees and elbows but failed to land anything really damaging.

Scott's arms were getting heavy too but he remembered to keep them up. His opponent was unconsciously lowering his guard as he tired.

Though his arms were feeling like lead, Scott knew that he had to keep planning his moves. A short right to the packer's ribs brought his guard a bit lower and like lightning Scott fired a right cross over the man's hands. It landed high on the bridge of Jarrett's nose and his forehead and it jarred Scott's hand but he knew that the punch would do its job. Two black eyes would result fairly quickly and with such limited vision, the tall packer was more susceptible to hooks and short body blows.

It was no time, though, for Scott to take chances

and he circled about, keeping out of trouble. Jarrett's face was a mess and his own felt only slightly better when the fight suddenly ended.

Hennessey and Macklin broke through the ring of spectators, seized the protagonists and pulled them apart.

'That's enough,' the sheriff bellowed as he grabbed Jarrett by the shoulders and swung him out of the way. 'The peace has been disturbed enough for one day.'

Macklin had seized Scott in a similar manner. 'Take it easy,' he said. 'The fight's over.' Then he added quietly, 'We waited until you gave that sonofabitch a good hammering before we stopped it.'

The onlookers moaned in disappointment and the fighters glared at each other, but around Crossville Hennessey's word was law and all knew that this fight was over. Few doubted, however, that the animosity between the pair would soon break out again at another time or place.

Rafe Gilmore then joined them, growling, 'It's lucky tomorrow's Sunday and I don't need either of you pair. But on Monday, anyone who doesn't turn up for work is fired.'

As Scott headed for the pump at the corral to wash off some of the blood, he passed Maley. The latter made no comment and just fixed him with the cold stare that seemed to be his habitual expression.

He was sluicing away some of the marks of battle when Macklin walked up to him. 'You were making catsmeat of Jarrett,' he said casually. 'But we didn't want you breaking your gun hand on his hard skull because chances are you're going to need it.'

Without waiting for any comment from a very surprised Scott, the deputy strolled away.

ELEVEN

Next morning it would have been hard to convince Scott that he had won the fight, despite what a few onlookers had told him. He was bruised in places where he could not remember being hit and derived little satisfaction that his hands were sore from pounding Jarrett. The encounter might have earned him a bit more respect, but he doubted that he had gained the affection of his fellow workers.

Mainly to get away from the town and the curious looks he was attracting, he saddled his horse after breakfast, hoping that a ride might leave him more clear-headed as regards the circumstances in which he had found himself.

Corporal Wade, always an early riser, wandered over from the tents that were the soldiers' new accommodation. He smiled and said, 'Howdy, champ. You gave Jarrett a well-deserved whipping yesterday.'

'If I'm the winner, I'd hate to be the loser,' Scott

replied as he mounted the horse. 'I'm going for a ride to try to loosen up a bit. Yesterday was not my idea of fun.'

The corporal laughed. 'Enjoy your ride. At least you have the day off. Lieutenant Cowell has a few jobs mapped out for us today. We are getting ready for the move to Fort Harris. There's no need for us here now.'

Scott cantered down the empty street and turned his mount south on the main trail. He had no special destination in mind and was mainly interested in open ground where the horse could get a degree of light exercise. He did not feel up to anything energetic.

He soon cleared the more settled areas close to the town, following the unfamiliar road just to see where it led. Gradually the houses thinned out and the presence of corrals and fenced horse pastures told him that he was riding into grazing country. Some of the ranches were not big, but they still had considerable numbers of stock feeding on the open range that lay further to the south.

As he topped a small rise, he saw a rider coming from a ranch house that, with a cluster of out-buildings, was situated about half a mile back from the main trail. There was something familiar about the small person on the shiny black pony.

Mary recognized the bay horse even before she could identify its rider. When she did, she halted her pony beside the mailbox, which had been her original destination. The smile of recognition on her face changed to one of concern as Scott's bruised face became more discernible.

Fighting back curiosity, she greeted him. 'Hello, Scott, out for a morning ride?'

'Howdy, Mary. I just thought I'd get out of town for a while. I don't like towns much and some of the folks in them I like even less.'

'It looks as though someone there might have taken a dislike to you, too.'

'I had a bit of a run-in with Lije Jarrett. The sheriff broke it up before things got too serious, but the trouble between us is still there. I reckon, though, that Jarrett might think twice about a return bout. Around about now, I reckon he's feeling a bit worse than me.'

Concern showed on the girl's face and in the tone of her voice as she told him, 'Be careful, Scott. Jarrett is known to be a murderer although he somehow managed to get himself acquitted in court. You have enough enemies at present. The McRaes tell me that there is a lot of talk in town about that pack-train ambush and the fire at the stores depot. Rumours are flying about Crossville that you know the people behind all that. I have heard that you are secretly a lawman and others say that you are a member of an outlaw gang.'

'Those stories are wrong. If I knew anything I would have told Hennessey or Maley, the government investigator. There's something going on, but nobody's telling me anything. The couple of characters who proved to be involved were all complete strangers to me. I don't know of any link between the ambush of the pack train and the burning of the stores depot.' Then suddenly he paused as his memory stirred, before continuing: 'I just had an idea. You mentioned once that you had seen a rider on a buckskin horse with this horse's rider at the stores depot.'

'I did. Why?'

'I was out with Maley a couple of days ago. We found the rider of that buckskin dead. He was wounded earlier and his partners shot him when they saw us coming and he couldn't be moved. There's the link with the depot and it's more suspicious that nobody there claimed to know the two men involved. If they were regular visitors, somebody knew them. I'm caught in the middle of all of this and I'm getting mighty sick of being used by people who know a lot more than they're prepared to tell me.'

'What are you going to do?'

He answered, 'I'll figure out something. I'm not sure what, but I'm getting sick of it all.'

'Come home with me and have a cup of coffee,' Mary suggested. 'It sounds like you could do with some friends.'

Scott accepted with alacrity and spent an enjoyable hour talking with the Hegartys. He tried to keep the conversation away from all the recent violence and sensing his reluctance, the others stifled their curiosity and confined the conversation to ranching and livestock. He started to relax for the first time in many days, but knew that he had to return to Crossville. Thanking his hosts and accepting an invitation to visit again, he took his leave.

'Be careful of that Mr Maley,' Mary warned. 'From what the McRaes tell me, he has a bad reputation. The word around town is that he always finds someone when he investigates and as long as he gets a conviction, he does not worry about guilt or innocence.'

As he mounted his horse, he told her, 'Don't worry. I trust no one except maybe for you folks. Thanks again. It's been nice to relax for a while.'

Glancing over his shoulder, he was pleased to see Mary smiling and waving as he cantered away.

'Sure is some girl,' he told his horse as they turned back towards the town.

Two miles from the ranch, Scott came across three riders who were studying hoof tracks on the trail. Mose Dodge had been worried that their intended victim might have already passed as they were a bit late getting on his tracks, but was reassured by the knowledge that they were still between Scott and Crossville.

It had taken a while for Mort Stawell to relay the orders from Crossville to the other pair who were lying low in a secure hideout. The orders themselves were simple: kill Scott Bailey before he returned to town.

Luther was enthusiastic about the idea and actually smiled while cradling a Sharps & Hankins .50-calibre carbine in his arms. He had been promised the next modern repeater the gang could steal, but at present he was stuck with a well-worn, Civil War surplus weapon. In a rare show of initiative, he had appropriated the buckskin horse formerly ridden by Dawson. It was no better than his original mount, but he preferred the horse's colour.

Mort Stawell was the third member of the party, a thin, flashily dressed young man with a lean, almost gaunt face and narrow, critical eyes. He had been a small-time rustler and in an effort to earn more respect on the criminal scene, sported a pair of pearl-handled Colts that he hoped might attract suitable customers who might launch his new career as a hired gun. Dodge had assured him that disposing of Scott would bring him to notice as a man to be feared.

Secretly, though, Dodge had a few misgivings about the ability of his two henchmen. Luther was a bumbling type and he feared that Stawell might not be the nerveless man-killer he was pretending to be. Three against one were good odds, but given the toll he had already taken on the gang, it would not pay to take Scott too lightly.

The planned ambush would be simple. Luther would take the first shot with his carbine. He was a good marksman and had selected a position from which he could take a straight-on shot at the approaching rider from about fifty yards. His companions would conceal themselves beside the trail in a position from where they could ride out quickly to attack their victim if Luther's shot did not disable or kill him.

Stawell was keeping watch around a bend in the trail and suddenly came galloping back. 'He's coming. Should be here soon.'

'Get to your places,' Dodge ordered. 'Luther, you shoot when he comes almost opposite Mort and me. Don't miss.'

The younger gunman gave a confident smile. 'Don't worry, Mose. I don't miss very often with this old gun. That fella is in for a hell of a shock.'

TWELVE

Scott saw nothing unusual when he first rounded the bend in the trail. Almost directly in front of him, about a hundred yards further on, were a couple of large boulders partially screened by brush. Much closer, but to his right, stood a massive boulder fully ten feet in height while on his left the trail was bordered by low brush.

He was only a few yards from the boulder on the right when a slight breeze carried a scent to the horse; the animal, detecting more of its own kind, momentarily halted, snorted and looked to the right. It was then that the rider noticed fresh hoofprints in the soft ground at the side of the trail.

Seeing his target hesitate, Luther threw the carbine to his shoulder, sighted quickly and squeezed the trigger. The hammer fell with a click as it struck the soft copper rim of the cartridge. Misfires were relatively common with rimfire ammunition because occasionally the priming compound did not go completely around the interior base of the shell.

Frantically, Luther cocked the rifle and tried again. Once more the cartridge failed to explode so he slid forward the barrel to extract the faulty bullet and insert a new one.

By now Scott was fully alert and though looking to his right, he caught the sign of movement ahead from the corner of his eye. Wheeling the bay horse about, he spurred back the way he had come.

Dodge and Stawell heard the sounds of Scott's retreat, saw Luther high above his rock reloading his carbine, and knew that they had lost the element of surprise. 'After him!' Dodge yelled as he urged his mount on to the trail and turned it after the fleeing rider.

To escape the rifleman's line of fire, Scott swung his horse off the trail so that the nearby boulder would screen him. The red earth was mostly covered by low sagebrush and he saw no obstacle in his path until the bay horse galloped into a concealed rabbit warren and crashed down as the ground collapsed beneath its weight. The landing was hard but fortunately the horse did not fall on him.

Breaking his fall with his hands, Scott rolled a few yards in the sage before coming to a stop. The sight of two riders bearing down on him had him clawing for the Colt that fortunately had stayed in his holster.

Dodge was on his left front and Stawell was on his companion's right which meant that only the former could get a clear shot at the man on the ground and he had to twist to his left to do it.

Scott fired first and thought he had missed, but then saw Dodge carried past him as he was unable to check his horse. Though he did not know it, the bullet had clipped the point of his target's left shoulder, rendering his bridle hand useless. As the out-of-control horse surged ahead, it exposed Stawell, who also found himself at a disadvantage. With his savage spade bit, he jerked his horse to an open-mouthed sliding stop and fired wildly as Scott's gun muzzle swung at him and spat flame. The impact of the heavy .45 slug hitting his side knocked him halfway from his saddle and as the horse shied away from the blast, it dislodged him.

Scott put another bullet into him almost as soon as he hit the ground. The range was short and with the odds against him, he was in no mood to spare someone who might still be able to kill him.

By this time Luther had mounted to join the fray, but he saw Dodge apparently fleeing the scene and Stawell's riderless horse standing tangled in its reins. Lacking further instructions on what he was supposed to do, he gave Scott a wide berth and galloped after Dodge.

Stawell was no longer a threat and remained sprawled face down where he had fallen. The second shot had been unnecessary, although Scott did not know that at the time. Picking up the dead man's guns, he stuck them in his belt and went to catch his horse. The animal's sweaty hide was caked with red dirt, but it seemed none the worse for its fall.

Keeping a sharp eye out for the two missing gunmen, he led his horse to where Stawell's mount was waiting and collected it. He was hoping to find a rifle in the saddle scabbard as he had left his recently acquired Winchester back at the mule corrals. Like most cowhands, he did not like burdening his horse with unnecessary weight that also unbalanced the saddle. He had not foreseen any trouble when he had set out for his ride. Now, in case the others should appear, he wanted some means of keeping them at a distance. He was disappointed, though, because the weapon on Stawell's saddle turned out to be a short-barrelled shotgun with little more effective range than the revolvers he had collected.

He decided to leave Stawell where he was, but would take his horse and weapons to deny their use to his criminal associates. While still wondering if he should attempt to cover the body, some movement on a distant ridge caught his eye. The buckskin horse was easy to see and a darker-coloured one was partially visible above the ridge line, certain proof that his late attackers had not forgotten him.

Pale, in great pain and very angry, Dodge had dismounted and sat on a rock while Luther showing rare wisdom decided to give him a wide berth. He was acting as a lookout, fearing that Scott might follow up the advantage he had gained. 'Looks like he's takin' Mort's horse,' he called to the wounded man. 'He ain't comin' this way. Do you reckon we should go after him?'

'What makes you think our chances would be better now with me wounded and Stawell probably dead? You had a good chance at him and you messed it up.'

'That wasn't my fault. If I'd had a decent repeater, I could have thrown out that dud rimfire and killed him with the next shot.'

'Kill him? After your performance today, I wouldn't bet you could hit your finger if it was shoved down the rifle barrel. Keep watching that sonofabitch because if he comes after us, we could be in trouble.'

'I'd like to see him try,' Ashton said. 'This time I'll borrow your Winchester and do the job right.'

Reluctant to waste any more breath, Dodge just scowled at him.

Scott did not know that Dodge was wounded and drew a little comfort from the fact that his remaining attackers seemed to be giving him a wide berth. He was a little surprised at their apparent lack of resolve, but was still worried that the pair could be waiting for reinforcements before they came after him again.

Had he not recognized the buckskin horse he might have thought that his attackers were simply road agents, but now he was sure that he had been specially targeted. He could only guess that revenge for the men he had killed was the most likely motive as he knew practically nothing of the incidents that Maley was investigating. What he did know was that he had been used. To lure the killers from cover, Maley and the lawmen had used him as bait probably by attributing to him information that he did not have. It was only by chance that he had survived the most recent encounter and there was no doubt that somebody in Crossville knew where to find the gunmen and tell them where he was. Feeling angry, he was in no mood to play the lethal games his enemies intended for him.

He removed the dead man's gunbelt, placed the twin revolvers in their holsters and looped the belt around his saddle horn. The shotgun was loaded and he collected two more buckshot cartridges from the pocket of Stawell's fancy Mexican jacket. By the time he had the two horses ready to move, he saw no sign of his late attackers, which did little for his peace of mind. Were they circling around somewhere in the hope of setting a new ambush?

Mounting quickly he led the riderless horse back towards Crossville. He had no intention of trying to take the dead man with him. That was the law's job and in his present mood he had no urge to make the task any easier for those who had put him in this danger.

Stawell's horse was easily led and Scott was moving at a steady canter when he topped a slight rise and saw another rider approaching from the direction of town. The sun glinted on the barrel of a rifle the man was carrying and the rider was clearly approaching at speed.

Scott dropped the reins of the led horse and brought up the shotgun so that the butt rested on his thigh. His action would have been visible to the oncoming rider, but the latter never slowed his mount's pace.

As the rider came nearer, Scott recognized Macklin, Hennessey's deputy, but he was no longer sure of whom he could trust. He slipped his right thumb over one of the gun's big rabbit-ear hammers and waited.

Macklin had recognized Scott, but the latter's aggressive pose made him a little wary. He slowed his approach and moved forward cautiously because he was not expecting such an unfriendly reaction.

'It's Tom Macklin, Bailey. Be careful with that gun,' he called. 'I heard shooting. What's happening?'

'Three men tried to bushwhack me. I got one but the other two are still about. What are you doing out here?'

'I heard from someone in town that they had seen a man named Stawell riding out this way. I have a warrant for him on horse-stealing charges. I thought I'd see if I could catch up with him. That horse you're leading fits the description of the one he was said to be riding.'

'Then you aren't out here looking to keep me out of trouble?'

'I didn't even know that you had left Crossville. Now let's have a look at the man you shot.'

'Be careful. His two *compadres* are still around here somewhere.'

Macklin gave a grim smile. 'If they are Mose Dodge and Luther Ashton, we won't have too much to worry about. They used to hang about with Stawell. I'm not scared of them.'

'You mightn't be,' Scott admitted, 'but they sure scared me. I reckon I need to keep a sharp eye out, seeing as the law ain't particularly interested in my welfare.'

The deputy ignored the barbed comment. 'You can watch out for them while I get the dead man across his horse so we can show Sheriff Hennessey your latest victim. If you keep going the way you are we might need to enlarge the graveyard.'

'Just as long as you don't make extra room for me,' Scott replied.

THIRTEEN

Few people were about when the deputy and Scott arrived back in town with Stawell's body, but word spread quickly. When Scott left the sheriff's office an hour later he found a small crowd had gathered outside.

'What's happening?' a man asked.

Scott unhitched his horse from the rail and replied, 'Ask Hennessey,' as he led the mount away. He was tired of this unfriendly town and people who asked questions, but told him little.

Wade found him just as he had finished feeding his horse. 'You look like you could do with a drink,' the corporal said with a smile.

The soldier had guessed right, but Scott declined. It was almost two weeks until he was paid and his cash reserves were running low.

Wade looked at him shrewdly. 'I've been in the army long enough to spot a man short of money. You don't need to worry. I won a bottle of whiskey in a card game and am looking for someone to share it with. I'm the only one on duty now. I reckon all the others who have finished are at the saloon anyway. We have the whole place to ourselves.'

'Are you allowed to drink on duty?'

'Hell, no. But what that Jackass Cowell don't know, sure as hell ain't gonna hurt him. I can see all that I need to see just by looking out the barn window.'

'In that case you can talk me into it,' Scott replied. 'Lead the way.'

Seated on bales of hay in the barn, they spent a relaxing hour talking. Inevitably the conversation swung around to Maley and his investigation.

'It looks like Hangman Maley won't be around much longer,' Wade said as he sloshed a bit more whiskey into his tin cup. Then, in a conspiratorial tone, he continued, 'I ain't supposed to tell anyone, but we got word last night by telegraph. A cavalry patrol picked up two men with our stolen mules. Neither was inclined to surrender and both managed to get themselves killed. Counting the ones you got, I reckon that's the end of the gang. They won't ambush any more pack trains. There might be a few of the less important crooks about, but the sheriff will probably pick them up. Anyway Maley's job is over.'

'What happened to the stuff that was stolen? Was that recovered?'

'No. They must have sold it or stashed it somewhere, but it won't do them any good now.'

'What about the fire that destroyed the depot?'

Wade shrugged his shoulders. 'My guess is that poor old Arthur Meade probably dropped a cigarette while he was sleeping off his latest skinful. He never could hold his liquor, but at least we won't have to cover up for him any more. Cowell never did like drunks.'

'Have you heard what's going to happen to the pack train?'

Wade took another sip of his whiskey. 'It ain't official yet, but I guess we will all go back to the main base at Fort Harris. The rest of my regiment is there and our men and mules will bring the pack train up to full strength again. I won't be sorry to leave this place.'

'Me neither,' Scott declared. Then he remembered Mary Hegarty and suddenly had the impression that he might have spoken too soon.

The next day Gilmore called his packers together. First he singled out Scott and Jarrett and bluntly told them that their fight was over and that they would work together without animosity. If either objected to that ruling they were free to go, but if they stayed on and trouble broke out again, both would be fired. Then he announced that the outfit would be moving at the month's end. Soldiers, packers, mules and their remaining equipment would be transferred to Fort Harris. This news came as no surprise as all could see that their presence in Crossville was no longer needed.

Immediately the packers set to work. Some mules needed to be shod; there were packs to be repaired and made ready and rubbish to be burned. The latter task fell to Scott. It was not the most enjoyable work, but he had done worse. The rubbish, mostly paper and empty boxes, was loaded into a light two-mule wagon which Scott would drive to an erosion gully a short way from town. There he would empty the wagon's contents and burn them. He was to remain close to the fire and ensure that it was burned out before leaving it for another load. With the right wind, sparks could be carried to places where they could start other fires. Crossville did not need a repeat episode of the stores depot fire.

Staring idly at the fire seemed to trigger something in Scott's mind, something that had been nagging at him for a few days. He remembered the traces of the fire he had seen in the mountains. At the time it had made little sense to him that the the supplies should have been unpacked, the original containers burned, and the mules repacked again. By then the thieves might have been aware that he had escaped and was likely to bring help. Their actions made little sense until suddenly Scott had an idea. At first it had seemed ridiculous, but when all aspects were considered together, pieces of the puzzle started falling into place.

The next problem would be in gaining acceptance for his theory. Whom should he tell? He would have preferred to inform Hennessey and Macklin, but certain details seemed to him to be outside their jurisdiction. The alternative was Maley and he was more than a little troubled by the man's reputation. Would he use any information for his own purposes to the detriment of his informant?

Scott was sure that he had been used as bait to bring the pack train raiders out into the open. The events of the previous day had done little to change his opinion. The discomforting thought came to him that in his present situation he could easily be ambushed. Two of the gang were still at large and somewhere an unknown person was directing them. Was it Cowell or Jarrett or both?

Reluctantly he reached the conclusion that Maley would be the appropriate person to approach because of the military involvement.

Before returning to the mule corrals, he paused at McRae's store long enough to buy writing materials, a strong brown paper envelope and a pencil. While the next load of trash was burning, he wrote down his conclusions and hoping they were right, sealed them in the envelope. On his return to Crossville, he asked Joan McRae to give the envelope to Mary Hegarty when next she came to town.

'Writing love letters, Scott?' Joan teased.

'I wish it was, but if anything should happen to me before Mary comes to town, I want you to give this envelope to Sheriff Hennessey.'

Joan looked concerned by his serious tone. 'Is anything wrong? It sounds like this is a very important matter. Are you in any trouble?'

'No, but I want someone I could trust to know what has happened if things go wrong. Just a bit of insurance.'

'This sounds very serious. Can my husband or I help you?'

'Thanks, Mrs McRae, but it is safest that you don't get involved. If you just take care of that envelope and tell nobody about it, that will be a great help.'

Back at the mule corrals the others had finished work for the day. He was unhitching the mules when Wade arrived. 'I'll put the feed out for your team while you groom them and put the harness away. It seems that you don't have a lot of friends among the other packers. None of them waited around to help you when their work was over.'

'Thanks. I'd appreciate the help. It seems I will always be an outsider with this crew. Has anything exciting happened while I was away burning trash?'

'Maley was asking around for you. He wants to see you about something or other. He's a sneaky sonofabitch. Be careful of him.'

They talked casually for a while, finished the work and then headed for the rough shed that served as a cookhouse for both the civilian and military members of the camp.

The army cook was grumpy at being delayed by late arrivals. The stew was getting cold, but at least there was fresh bread and the coffee tasted good. The pair ate and then went their separate ways.

Scott was wondering where he would find Maley when the latter found him. The investigator was standing in the dark shadows and called to him softly as he walked to the barn. 'Bailey – over here.'

'You wanted to see me?'

'Yes. I've heard Macklin's version of what happened yesterday. Now I want to hear your version.'

'Playing one against the other, are you?'

'No, but no two witnesses see exactly the same thing and one might forget something important. I'm not out to trap anyone.'

'That's good, because I've been doing a bit of thinking and have a few ideas about that ambush of the pack train. You might not believe them, but they make sense to me.'

'Go ahead. I might ask you a question or two but I am prepared to hear anything that might be helpful.'

'Supposing I say that certain people here had arranged to have the pack train ambushed. They set up a stranger and a drunk packer so as not to upset the locals too much when they were killed. Ed Newton and I were not supposed to come back.'

'Why?'

'Because that pack train was carrying empty boxes and trash. It would have been discovered when we went to unpack the mules. That's why the mules were loaded when I arrived to start work. Cowell and Jarrett and probably some of the others were working in cahoots. I know some mules can be smart but I've never seen any smart enough to pack themselves.

106

Find who packed the mules and you should soon find those behind this whole deal. One man could not have organized this. Seems to me there are two separate gangs, the military and some mighty bad civilians. The army side had regular contacts with the ambushers and I know that some of them were actually seen around the mule corrals.'

'Who told you that?'

'At this stage the name is not important, but I got that good bay horse from a man who was sent from town to kill me the night the stores depot was burned. Let's say a horse-loving informant of mine had noticed the horse at the mule corrals. That buckskin horse we were chasing in the mountains was there too. The dead man we found in the mountains was riding it when I killed the bay horse's owner. I saw that same horse yesterday under another rider during an attempted ambush on the road. Those would-be killers had friends at the mule corrals.'

'But why would they want to steal an empty pack train? The mules would bring a good price, but it would not be much when the money was split up among the number of people involved.'

'Don't play dumb with me, Maley, I think you have already figured the answer to that and that's why you were sent out here. The pack train and the destruction of the stores depot were meant to account for serious shortages of military supplies that were probably sold on the civilian market. Am I right?'

The investigator shrugged his shoulders and

admitted, 'You are right. Although the Civil War ended ten years ago, military stores are still bulging with surplus equipment of all kinds. Today's much-reduced army cannot use a fraction of it. That is why some cavalry regiments still have outdated Civil War uniforms and equipment. There are so many McClellan saddles in stores that the army has enough to take them well into next century. The McClellan is by no means a perfect saddle, but no new designs will be seriously considered until current stocks are used up or reduced. There are thousands of rifled muskets that cannot be sold except illegally to Indians or as scrap iron, but there are many other items that bring good money on the civilian market. Medical supplies, tools, certain instruments like com-passes, boots, blankets and tents are all worth good money on the civilian market and winter-issue buffalo coats are worth more than two months' pay for the average soldier. Pilfering equipment from army stores is rife. Sometimes it is small scale just to earn a bit of drinking money, but in other cases, it is a very lucrative, highly organized business and that's what we have here. You were a marked man because the gang thought that sooner or later you would start remembering some of the many irregularities about that train. And I must admit that I encouraged the same idea. I needed something to bring these people out into the open.'

'Even if it meant my getting shot full of holes. You knew about this all along,' Scott accused.

'Not all of it and I was trying to watch your back. Your information has supplied a lot more pieces to this puzzle.'

'Surely you have enough evidence now to act.'

'Not quite. I want this case to be tied up nicely because we are looking at murder and attempted murder as well as wholesale theft. I thought I had the evidence, but it was destroyed in the fire along with one of my best men.'

'Do you mean that Meade fella?'

'The same. I know he is being blamed for the fire, but he was not the careless drunk that Cowell described and he never smoked. Arthur Meade was murdered and I intend to get his killer.'

'So you reckon Cowell is behind all this?'

'Probably. I think it is time to press him a little and see what happens.'

'Don't forget the others,' said Scott. 'There had to be more than just Cowell in this. Somebody packed a dozen mules with boxes and bales that were empty or full of trash. Jarrett was there and I remember him saying that they had help from Cowell's men. Newton could have been helping and been so drunk he was not taking much notice. Round up the men who packed those mules and you have closed this end of their operations. I'm quite happy to give you a hand when you decide to have things out with this bunch. Call me narrow-minded but I take it personally when someone tries to kill me. If you want a bit of help you can have my services for nothing. What do you say?'

'Chances are I'll need you. Just stay around and don't say a word of this to anyone. Without each other, you and I are mighty short of friends.'

FOURTEEN

Next morning, Maley sought out the lieutenant and started asking him a few questions about the store inventory before the fire as well as pressing him for details of the equipment lost with the pack train. The soldier soon began to flounder quickly and could only plead ignorance due to the loss of all records. Those working around the corral heard the investigator's raised voice, a direct contrast to the low, controlled tone he habitually used.

Scott was feeding the mules when Wade joined him. Looking unusually cheerful, the corporal chuckled. 'Sounds like the hangman is giving Cowell a pretty rough time. It's nice to see that sonofabitch squirming for a while. I was never one of the lieutenant's favourites because I queried some of the stock records. Something was wrong, but Cowell didn't want to know about it. Now I'm beginning to know why. Do you reckon our leader could be looking at a court martial for all this?'

111

'I wouldn't know,' Scott answered. 'Nobody around here tells me anything. I think they must be annoyed with me for not getting killed and causing all this fuss.'

'You could be right at that,' Wade told him before wandering away to eavesdrop the conversation in the shed.

The rest of the day was busy as pack saddles and other pieces of harness were collected, inventoried and stowed in one of the two wagons that would be used to shift the packer's possessions. A third wagon was loaded with fodder for the journey and surplus grain was fed to the stock to build them up for the eighty-mile journey to the rest of the train. The mules not needed to pull the wagons would be loose herded.

Gilmore estimated that the journey would take three days without excessively tiring the stock. He seemed to have renewed his interest in how his men were progressing. In anticipation of more interesting work free from a town existence, the boss packer was taking a more active role and leaving less of the team's running to Jarrett. He was quietly pleased that he would soon be out patrolling with the cavalry again. The sooner he was clear of Crossville the better he would like it.

To his mind, the whole sorry episode was beginning to clear up. Most of the men involved in the ambush were dead and the sheriff was confident that Dodge and Ashton would soon be apprehended. Life at Fort

Harris would be busier, but much less complicated.

When work finished for the night the packers ate and most headed for the saloon for a final drink, Scott felt, though, that he would not be welcome in the gathering and was almost broke into the bargain.

He was walking aimlessly around town when he met the Hegarty family, who were just saying goodbye to the McRaes at the door of the store.

'Hello, Scott,' Joan McRae greeted. 'I thought you would be at the saloon celebrating your departure tomorrow.'

'If we had known you were at a loose end, we could have invited you to dinner with us,' her husband said.

Mary sounded a little disappointed as she asked, 'Is it true that you are leaving Crossville tomorrow? I only heard about it at dinner tonight. Joan gave me that letter you sent me to hold. What do you want me to do with it?'

'I know this sounds a bit dramatic, but if anything happens to me in the next couple of days, I want you to give the letter to Sheriff Hennessey. Meanwhile, don't open it or tell anyone else about it.'

McRae sounded surprised. 'I didn't think things were as serious as that. Has it been confirmed that the entire Gilmore crew are leaving Crossville?'

'That's right. With the army store gone there's no need for our team so we're going to join the rest of the train at Fort Harris. Things are happening pretty fast now.'

113

'You won't be coming back this way?' Mary made no effort to hide her disappointed tone.

'Who knows? I'm a cowhand by trade and this packing work is just another job. The people I'm working with here are different from cowboys and I'm not sure that I'll ever fit in.'

'At least there'll be more people at the fort. I'm sure you'll find more friends there,' Susan Hegarty told him soothingly.

The sound of a shot stopped all further conversation.

'Someone's shooting,' Bill Hegarty said.

Joan McRae laughed. 'Probably some drunk trying to shoot out the lights in the saloon. More work for Sheriff Hennessey.'

Scott disagreed. 'That shot came from the mule corrals. I think I'll take a look. Excuse me, folks.'

He had hurried about fifty yards away before he realized that he had not said goodbye to his friends, but it was too late to turn back. As he passed the hotel, Maley appeared hatless and coatless, but hastily buckling on his gunbelt.

Barely glancing at Scott he muttered, 'Sounds like trouble at the packers' camp. If you're coming with me keep your eyes open.'

FIFTEEN

They were first to reach the scene. A lamp was burning in the makeshift office and the smell of burnt powder still hung in the air as Maley threw open the door. The lieutenant lay on the floor, but blood and part of his brain had spattered the wall beside the improvized desk he had been using. An army Colt .45 was lying near his right hand.

Scott looked over Maley's shoulder and in his surprise stated what looked terribly obvious. 'He's killed himself.'

The investigator did not reply, but knelt and picked up the still-warm gun. He opened the loading gate to find one fired shell and five empty chambers. Macklin arrived panting from a long run. 'What's going on?'

'Looks like Cowell shot himself.' Maley passed the gun to the deputy as he spoke. 'He did a pretty thorough job of it too.'

Macklin glanced at the dead man and examined

the weapon. 'Only one bullet in the gun. Looks like he loaded it specially to do the job. Used an army Schofield slug and sure as hell didn't miss. Why would he want to do that?'

'Because I was asking him a lot of difficult questions about missing government stores and a murder or two.'

'That could explain it,' Macklin admitted.

While the deputy familiarized himself with the scene, Maley picked up the officer's pistol belt and holster which had been lying on an empty box in the corner of the room. He opened the cartridge pouch and tipped the contents into his hand. They made quite a handful and he was forced to drop the pouch and hold them in his cupped hands, 'Count these and tell me what brands they are,' he snapped at Scott.

The latter resented being ordered about, but decided that the gravity of the situation accounted for Maley's lack of manners. He did as he was told, counting the cartridges back into the pouch. 'Eighteen,' he said as he secured the billet holding the flap. 'All army Colt .45s.'

'You're sure?'

'I'm sure. I can count to eighteen, but count them yourself if you're not happy.'

If Maley heard him, he gave little indication. Instead he turned to the deputy. 'We might not be looking at a suicide here.'

Macklin was in no mood to play games. 'You can't

mean this was an accident.'

'It could be murder. A soldier's usual issue of pistol ammunition is eighteen rounds. Cowell had his eighteen bullets in his cartridge pouch. He kept his pistol unloaded when not in the field and I reckon that if he wanted to shoot himself, he would have taken one of the rounds issued to him. He had Colt cartridges. The slug that killed him was a Smith & Wesson .45 originally intended for the Schofield revolver.'

The deputy was interested, but far from convinced. 'But the army tried a few Schofields and the Schofield bullet fits the army Colt. Cowell was a stores officer and would have had access to all sorts of ammunition.'

'That's true. They issued quite a few Schofields, but finally recalled them because the top-break loading system could cause a man reloading on horseback to drop live rounds along with empty shells. They sold the guns as surplus and a lot were bought for Wells Fargo messengers. The ammunition could still be used, though, and a lot was issued to the troops.'

'You could have a point, Maley, but the fact of the matter is that the army still has a lot of that ammunition and a stores officer might have picked some up in his travels.'

'There're are a lot of civilians who use that ammunition too,' Scott volunteered. 'You can buy it in most places these days. It fits the Colt, it's just a bit shorter.

117

The Colt cartridge is too long for the Schofield, though.'

At that moment Sheriff Hennessey arrived accompanied by Rafe Gilmore. He took in the scene briefly and asked Macklin, 'What happened?'

'Looks like Cowell shot himself. Maley here thinks that it might be murder. Cowell was shot with his own gun, but the bullet was a Schofield .45, not the Colt ammunition that the lieutenant had in his pouch. We know the army uses both types – it might be an idea to look at that angle.'

If the sheriff agreed, he did not say so and began to cast an experienced eye around the room. He had seen such sights before in places where guns and hard liquor mixed. In the absence of the latter he concluded that Cowell had been sober and asked about any suicide note. When told that no such note had been found, he appeared slightly puzzled. 'Usually when a sober person kills himself, he wants people to know why he did it.'

Gilmore had been silently studying the scene before finally asking the others, 'Why in blazes would Cowell want to shoot hisself? It ain't as if he was drunk and out of his mind.'

Maley offered a suggestion. 'He was in deep trouble over missing army stores, the ambush of the pack train and the fire at the depot. Two people were also murdered. I have been investigating his activities and let him know that I intended to nail his hide to the barn door as soon as I had enough evidence. He might have decided to take the easy way out.'

'If that's the easy way,' Gilmore muttered, 'I don't want to know about the hard way out.'

Suddenly Corporal Wade pushed his way into the room looking wide-eyed and obviously shaken. 'Well, I'll be damned, I never thought the lieutenant would go out this way. Did he really shoot himself?'

Hennessey's reply was guarded. 'Looks like it, but it's too soon to tell. It sure don't look like an accident.'

A crowd had gathered outside and after stating what he had seen for the record, Scott quickly left the shed. Bill Hegarty was among the onlookers and caught him by the arm. 'What's happened, Scott? Who was killed?'

Rather than risk starting a false rumour, Scott replied cautiously, 'Looks like Cowell shot himself. It's too soon to know any details. At this stage all the law is sure of is that the lieutenant is dead.'

The rancher sheepishly admitted that he was seeking information to inform his wife and daughter as well as the McRaes, who were waiting at the store. He bore a message to Scott from the store owners, that he was invited to join them at their place for a cup of coffee.

'I thought you folks would be on your way home,' Scott told him after trying not to look too eager about accepting the invitation.

The rancher explained that they had delayed their departure in the hope of learning more about the latest excitement. That was one aspect of town life that the Hegarty family missed; they saw more people in town on one day than they saw in two weeks on the ranch.

A short while later Scott found himself seated in a comfortable chair, drinking coffee from a china cup among polite and friendly company. Excepting the short visit to the Hegarty ranch, it was a long time since he had been in such luxury after so many cow camps and bunkhouses.

Aware that he was not entirely at home in such circumstances, Mary gently kept him in the conversation, asking his opinion on various subjects familiar to him. Soon he was enjoying himself and it was only with great reluctance that he excused himself. He explained that he would have to rise early and start feeding mules but was all too aware that it was getting late and the Hegartys were still faced with a long drive home.

'I'm not sure if we will be moving in the morning seeing as Lieutenant Cowell is out of the picture. Rafe Gilmore might wait until the law sorts out a few things.'

'So you might be with us for a while yet?' Mary said, hoping she did not appear too interested.

With equal pretence screening a degree of regret, Scott replied casually, 'Most likely, but I have given up trying to guess what is likely to happen around here.'

He would have liked to say goodbye to Mary in

private, but as she made no attempt to leave the others, he offered a mass farewell and headed for the door. He was about to close it behind him when he suddenly stopped and re-entered the room. In reply to their surprised looks he announced, 'I just remembered. There are two dangerous men still at large out your way. A buggy on a lonely road at night might tempt them to do something desperate. If you wait until I get my horse, I'll escort you home.'

'That won't be necessary,' the rancher said. 'I have a gun in my pocket, just in case.'

'That might not help you if they have rifles. I think I'd better come along. That pair could be anywhere and they sure are dangerous.'

Hegarty might have protested further, but his wife nudged him with her elbow. 'That's very kind of you, Scott. Those men could still be about and it's better to be sure than sorry. I had forgotten about them.'

Joan McRae quickly assessed the situation. She added, 'Susan's right, Bill. I think an escort is a very good idea. I want you to stay here until Scott gets his horse and comes back. Who knows what bad characters are lurking around here with all the strange things that have happened.'

Hegarty saw that he was outnumbered and gave in gracefully. 'Call back when you have your horse, Scott,' he chuckled. 'Meanwhile, Joan, you can give me another cup of coffee. That's the least you can do while you are holding me here.'

SIXTEEN

Ashton and Dodge scouted the ranch house carefully and made sure that it was empty before they broke through the back door. To fugitives deprived of life's comforts, it seemed like they had walked into a treasure trove. There was food in the pantry, coffee, clean linen to bandage Dodge's shoulder wound, and even a half-bottle of whiskey to dull the pain.

'We'd better not stay too long,' Ashton warned. 'These people might be comin' back.'

Dodge scoffed. 'If they were, they'd be back by now. I reckon they've gone overnight.' He continued, 'I'm not feeling too good with this shoulder the way it is. I might have a snort of whiskey and try for a couple of hours' shuteye when we have had some decent grub.'

'I ain't sure that's a good idea, Mose. What if them folks come back?'

'That would be their bad luck. I want you to keep a sharp eye out and wake me if you see or hear anything.

Meanwhile you can get some of that grub together to take with us. There's bread, biscuits, and bacon in the kitchen and take some salt too. If we have to live on game later, it tastes better with salt. You could fire up the stove and heat some water to clean up this shoulder when I wake up. We can use that tablecloth for bandages. There's a clock on the mantelpiece. Give me an hour and a half and start heating that water before you wake me. There should be some sort of stuff for patching up injuries somewhere. See if you can find that too.'

The Hegarty family knew something was wrong when they were still nearly half a mile from their house.

Bill reined up the team and pointed. 'There's smoke coming from the chimney and I can see a light in a front window. Someone's in our house.'

Scott turned his horse alongside the buckboard. 'I have a fair idea who it is. Don't come any closer in case someone starts shooting. Get your rig under cover and wait here. I'll creep up and see what I can see and then let you know.'

'I'll go with you,' Hegarty said.

'It's best you don't. Someone needs to guard the ladies. I'll leave my horse with you. If any shooting should start, head back to Crossville and get the law, pronto.'

The Hegarty family unanimously disagreed with the plan. It was their house, they argued, and they did not want to leave the problem to a comparative stranger. After a brief discussion, a compromise plan was reached. Scott would spy out the situation and if he confirmed the presence of the two gunmen, he would find a sheltered spot and briefly light a match. Upon seeing that signal, Mary would mount his horse and ride hard for Crossville. Her parents would remain under cover unless Bill felt it necessary to go to Scott's aid. The plan was far from perfect but at the time it had to suffice.

The approach to the ranch house offered plenty of cover in the way of trees and shrubs, but it could also conceal a sentry and there were places where Scott had to trust to luck. Movement between various patches of cover was made no easier by the thought that he could be moving into someone's gun sights. He knew that he was taking longer than expected and the Hegartys would be worried, but he resolved not to take any unnecessary risks.

Soon he could see two horses hitched to corral rails beside the house. Both were saddled and bridled and one was a buckskin. He knew immediately who would be in the cabin.

As quietly as he could, he made his presence known to the horses so they would not take fright and alarm their riders when he approached them. Talking softly he unhitched both and led them away from the building. When safely out of earshot, he unsaddled them and turned them loose to graze. Then with a clump of bushes shielding him from those in the house, he briefly lit a match. As this brought no response from the intruders, he knew that they were not keeping a proper watch.

Reassurance then came in the distant, faint sound of a galloping horse. Mary was on her way to town.

More confident now, Scott crept to the lighted window and risked a glimpse through the slightly open curtains. Ashton was dozing at the dining room table with the remains of hastily eaten food around him and an empty whiskey bottle nearby. Where was Dodge?

That question was answered by the clattering of an alarm clock. Ashton shook himself awake, rose, yawned and made his way to another room. Scott could hear voices as the two men talked. The voices got louder when the pair came into the dining room and Dodge saw the empty whiskey bottle.

'Damn you, Luther. I needed that whiskey. This arm is giving me hell.'

'I needed it too, I had to stay awake while you were takin' things easy. I'm just as tired as you are.'

'You ain't got a busted shoulder. Now start getting some stuff together. We have a heap of riding to do. The law's on to us and it's time we got going. The game's up with that army stuff now.'

'Do you reckon we should feed them horses we got outside? They'd be mighty dry by now too.'

Dodge growled at his companion. 'Ain't you got no sense at all? Them horses should have been watered and fed. We have some long, hard travel ahead of us. Now get out there and give them a small drink. See what grain they have and put enough for two feeds in a sack. We can't afford to stay around here too long. It's best we stop and feed them somewhere safe.'

Ashton was searching for a suitably offensive reply when he opened the front door, looked twice and gasped as though in disbelief, 'The horses – they're gone.'

'They can't be,' Dodge asserted. 'Probably just pulled away from where they were hitched. There's a fence right round this house and the corral. They'll be feeding around the place. Now get out there and find them.'

Scott heard the exchange and moved around the corner of the ranch house, drawing his gun as he did so. As Ashton rounded the corner, mumbling angrily to himself, he slammed the gun barrel down on his head. His victim fell immediately but in doing so knocked over a bucket left against the nearby wall.

Dodge heard the clatter and cursing his clumsy companion, lurched to the open door. As he peered out a hand grabbed his shirt front and jerked him forward. Almost simultaneously a gun barrel descended on his head and dropped him to his knees. As a reflex action he grabbed for his gun but his right arm was not functioning properly. Stunned though he was, the muzzle of a Colt .45 pressed against his head convinced him that such a move was likely to have fatal results.

'Touch that gun and you're dead,' Scott told him.

'My shoulder's busted,' Dodge snarled. 'I can't draw a gun.'

With his free hand Scott drew the other's gun and tucked it into his own belt. By this time Ashton had struggled to his hands and knees. Before he knew what was happening, another clout with a gun barrel knocked him flat and he too was relieved of his six-shooter.

As the pair struggled to regain their senses both became acutely aware that they could offer little by way of resistance.

'Both of you, walk or crawl away from the house. Get over there on that patch of grass and lie down. I don't want to mess up the house if I have to shoot you, but believe me, if one of you coyotes makes a wrong move, you're both dead.'

The prisoners knew he was not joking and nervously followed Scott's orders. Then he lit a match so that Bill Hegarty would know that he had the situation in hand. Even then the rancher had to be sure and halted in shouting range, but too far away for accurate night shooting. He called to Scott and only approached closer when the latter assured him that all was well.

They were still standing guard over their prisoners when Hennessey and Macklin arrived just before dawn.

Susan Hegarty was anxious to see how Mary had fared. Upon being assured that she was safe at McRae's she relaxed slightly, but was still anxious to see what damage had been done to their home. She climbed into the buckboard and drove up with the two lawmen.

The sheriff was tired and grumpy but his deputy was in good spirits and greeted the prisoners cheerfully. 'Nice to see you boys. I thought I'd have a lot of riding around before I caught up with you. Looks like Scott saved me the trouble.'

Dodge was in no mood for socializing. 'Shut your trap, Macklin. I'm hurt and I ain't in the mood to put up with your foolery.'

'You don't have to,' the deputy chuckled, 'but there's one mighty mean government man in Crossville waiting to have a little talk to you and your friend here. Ain't it nice to be so popular?'

Hennessey fitted handcuffs to both men, cuffing both of Ashton's wrists and connecting them to Dodge's left wrist. The wounded man's right wrist he left free after placing it in an improvised sling. Susan Hegarty had donated a piece of a worn but clean sheet for that purpose.

The sheriff arranged to borrow the Hegarty buckboard to transport the prisoners to town. He would drive while Macklin and Scott rode. The latter would take one of the prisoners' horses and lead the other. Mary Hegarty would return the vehicle when she went home.

The wounded Dodge did not enjoy the ride back to Crossville and moaned loudly at every bump on the rough road, but he received little sympathy.

'Stop complaining,' Hennessey told him. 'Think yourself lucky you're still alive.'

'I'll get you for this. You don't have anything on me.'

'Right now I can hold you on burglary charges, but if investigations show you were implicated in the death of Ed Newton or that soldier Meade, you'll both hang.'

Ashton turned pale. 'I wasn't a part of that. I just went along because I had to,' he protested.

The sheriff smiled to himself. He had found the weak link and was sure that Maley would soon extract plenty of evidence from the prisoner.

SEVENTEEN

Maley was far from happy when he emerged from the hotel dining room after breakfast. If a tasty breakfast had put him in a good mood, the sight of the procession coming down the street quickly reversed the situation. He would not have been surprised to see the two lawmen bringing in prisoners, but seeing Scott riding with them was an indication that he should have been involved. He had regarded the young packer as being tied to him and felt that he should have been informed before his star witness went out with a sheriff's posse. Impatiently he jammed on his hat and followed the party to the sheriff's office.

Hennessey was unloading his prisoners when the government man arrived. 'What's going on here?' he demanded.

The sheriff seemed pleased to see that he had stirred some sort of emotion in Maley. 'We have the last of your pack train ambushers here, caught 'em at

Hegarty's ranch last night. Didn't see any need to worry you as we were not sure what we had at first.'

'What's Scott Bailey doing with you? Why wasn't I told about this?'

Scott answered for himself. 'You don't own me, Maley. I was escorting the Hegartys home because these characters were still on the loose. As luck would have it, we found this pair at the ranch. I'm sure the sheriff would have called you if he thought you would be interested. Things happened mighty quick last night.'

'Don't get too upset, Maley,' Hennessey told the investigator. 'You can interview this pair in my jail any time you like. Look at it this way, you saved yourself a lot of extra riding and weren't pulled out of bed in the middle of the night like I was.'

Allowing himself a frosty smile, Maley replied, 'I suppose you're right, sheriff. You didn't need me as it turned out, but things could have been complicated if important witnesses got themselves killed.'

Macklin slapped Ashton on the shoulder. 'Did you hear that, Luther? For once in your life you're important.'

'Keep your mouth shut, Luther,' Dodge snarled. 'Don't say anything until you get a lawyer.'

'I don't know any lawyer, Mose.'

Macklin was enjoying the situation. 'If I was you I'd get the shyster who got Luke Jarrett off that murder charge but then, on second thoughts, you mightn't be able to afford him. If that's the case I'm sure the court will be able to sober up some broken-down lawyer to defend you, for all the good it will do. You and your friend here will finish up getting hung anyway.'

Dodge shouted to his thoroughly frightened accomplice, 'Keep your mouth shut. Don't say anything until we get a lawyer.'

Maley stood silently as the two prisoners were searched and placed in the cells. His stony features briefly relaxed into a fleeting smile, but then the poker face was there again. Ashton would talk, he knew that; but how much did he know?

At this point Scott called the sheriff aside and offered to see Mary Hegarty and arrange for her to return their family buckboard. He knew he would find her at McRaes'. Hennessey had no objections and, as he made for the door, Maley called after him. 'Don't go too far away, Bailey. I might need you later.'

Scott replied, 'I'm still working for Rafe Gilmore. See him when you want me. I'll drop the buckboard around for Mary Hegarty and find out what she has done with my horse. Then I'll be at the mule corrals.'

Bill Ruskin was a worried man. He had been on his way to work when he saw the sheriff arrive in town with his prisoners. He knew Ashton well and that he was not smart enough to conceal what he knew for long.

Ruskin had survived Maley's original questioning because he knew that the investigator was looking for bigger game. Things would be different now, though. The criminal gang was unravelling and as more information came to light, he would soon be implicated. After considerable thought he decided that if he left the area soon enough the extent of his involvement might be forgotten when the net closed on the bigger players.

As a single man living at a boarding-house, he had few possessions and he decided not to go back to collect what could easily and cheaply be replaced. Lacking his own horse, the quickest way out of town was on a government mule. It was safer than trying to steal a horse because if he was apprehended the government would show him less lenience than ordinary citizens who stole, and were still likely to be lynched for the same crime.

It was early and nobody had started work at the corrals when he caught and saddled a large mule that he knew was a good riding animal. He heaved a sigh of relief as he swung into his saddle. So far luck had been on his side.

Before he had ridden two yards, he heard his name called and the voice was the one he least wanted to hear.

Scott delivered the buckboard to the corral behind McRae's store and Mary was waiting when he drove up. She looked tired and Scott guessed that she had spent a restless, worried night.

He was quick to reassure her and described the

night's events. He was halfway through this when Joan McRae called from the kitchen window with an offer to join them at breakfast. Suddenly Scott became aware of how tired and hungry he was and wasted no time accepting the offer.

All too soon the meal was over and after some brief but heartfelt thanks to his hosts, he pushed back his chair and rose wearily to his feet.

Then they all heard the shot.

'Sounds like trouble again at the mule corral,' he said as he jammed on his hat. 'I might be needed.'

As matters developed Scott's prediction was wrong. Arriving at the corrals he found Jarrett, Corporal Wade and another soldier standing over a body on the ground. Getting closer he recognized the corpse as that of Bill Ruskin.

Jarrett was still holding a government Springfield carbine in his hand, He looked up angrily upon seeing Scott, but if he intended making any remarks, he didn't get the chance.

Macklin arrived running. He stopped a second to catch his breath and demanded, 'What's been happening here?'

Ignoring his companions, the packer replied, 'I shot Bill Ruskin. He was about to ride off on a government mule. I saw him and guessed he was stealing it. I grabbed a carbine and told him to stay where he was. He turned the mule my way and went for his gun. I got him dead centre. Corporal Wade was with me at the time. We were going over plans for the move when I saw Ruskin through the window. I loaded the carbine, and went to the door. When I told him to stop he went for his gun. That's all there is to it.'

The corporal knew the animosity between the pair and smiled ruefully when he was facing away from Jarrett before replying. 'It's true. Lije gave him a chance to surrender, but he went for a gun instead.'

Just then Maley joined the group and once again Jarrett had to describe what had happened. The investigator said little, but none doubted that he was weighing up the information. As usual his blank expression gave no indication of what he was thinking.

When Rafe Gilmore arrived Scott told him that he had been awake all night and was going to catch up on a few hours' sleep.

'You might as well,' the contractor said. 'The law will be questioning every man and his dog about the goings-on here recently. There's no point even starting any work today. We'll just feed and water the mules and leave it at that.' He continued, 'I never figured Ruskin for a thief and I thought he was too smart to go for his gun when Lije had the drop on him. Who would have thought there would be so much shooting and killing? I'd dearly like to know what's behind all this.'

'Did you try asking Maley?'

Gilmore snorted like an angry bull. 'That cold-hearted little sonofabitch wouldn't tell you where the door was if you were with him in a burning building.

I answer all his questions, but he tells me nothing and keeps everyone in the dark.'

Scott made no further comment and wearily made his way to the shed that served as a bunkhouse for the packers.

The sheriff, his deputy and Maley all questioned Jarrett at length but were unable to find evidence that Ruskin's killing was murder. The man's gun was near his body and Corporal Wade was considered an unbiased witness who only associated with Jarrett when it was necessary. Ruskin had been caught stealing the mule and it seemed likely that he was implicated in some of the recent crimes.

Hennessey ventured the opinion that the dead man had panicked when he saw Ashton and Dodge brought in alive.

Maley nodded. 'Makes sense. I knew Ruskin was holding something back, but am not sure of the extent of his involvement. Did he take an active part in the crimes or was he just someone who saw what was happening and kept his mouth shut?'

'We should find out more when we start questioning Dodge and Ashton,' the sheriff told him.

The investigator was not so confident, suggesting that Dodge would not talk and that Ashton would tell any lies that he thought would earn him leniency.

'Looks like this gang is falling apart,' Macklin told Maley.

The investigator said quietly, 'I think we have only cut the tail off the snake. Where is its head?'

Tired though he was, sleep did not come easily to Scott. More drama had occurred in the last couple of weeks than he had experienced in his entire life. Vaguely he remembered something that had puzzled him at the time, but had been pushed to the back of his mind by other, more urgent events. He was still trying to recall it when he finally drifted off to sleep.

Four hours later he awoke, washed and decided that a shave was in order. Then he changed into a clean but badly wrinkled shirt and ventured forth to find out the latest occurrences.

His first stop was Rafe Gilmore's office, but the contractor was missing. Next he went to the army camp, which was a hive of activity. Men were bustling about packing equipment and Corporal Wade was checking boxes and making notes. He paused when he saw Scott and said cheerfully, 'Here's the man of the hour. Is it right that you single-handedly captured the last of the pack train raiders? The talk is all over town.'

'Don't believe everything you hear. There were a lot of other people involved and I'm not sure they've all been rounded up yet. If you really want to know what's going on, I suggest you ask Maley.'

The soldier laughed. 'There's little chance that he would be prepared to satisfy idle curiosity. Secrecy, justified or not, is his middle name.'

'I wonder where all this fuss leaves me. I haven't

had much time with the pack train.'

'The whole outfit is moving back to join the rest of the train at Fort Harris. I think Gilmore means to take his whole crew. You might recall that he's lost a few packers lately. If you stay on, I reckon I'll see you at the fort. There are a couple of six-mule wagons coming to take us soldiers and most of the heavy stuff. Gilmore is going ahead by road in his buggy, but he told me the packers will bring the rest over the mountains on the mules. It should be an easy trip for you.'

'Nothing will be easy with Jarrett running things. I find it hard to believe that he isn't mixed up with what's been going on here.'

'You could be right,' Wade admitted. 'If Ashton and Dodge start talking they might implicate him. If that happens, he won't be going with you. If I was him I wouldn't want to hang around here too long while Maley's about. He has a reputation for tampering with evidence to make sure that his suspects are found guilty. People in Washington see him as a great investigator, but those working for the Quartermaster's Department take a very different view. Don't trust him an inch.'

EIGHTEEN

Jarrett was a hard man to frighten, but he had good reason to be scared. Thanks to the testimony of Corporal Wade, he had previously been able to evade a murder charge over the Ruskin killing, but he was a man with much to hide and there were lawmen circling like vultures.

Normally he was a methodical man who weighed major decisions carefully, but this time all his instincts were telling him to run. He had made all he was likely to make out of pilfering stores and had a money belt containing two thousand dollars in greenbacks: staying was no longer an option. He knew that the prisoners would talk, giving the lawmen enough evidence to put his neck squarely in a hangman's noose. His personal horse was in a corral with the privately owned animals and he wasted no time saddling it. Just as he was mounting, he saw Scott walk around the corner of a shed with his saddle on his shoulder.

They exchanged mutually hostile looks, but neither spoke. Anger seethed in Jarrett and he felt the urge to draw his gun and finish this person who had caused him so much trouble. He realized, however, that such a move could jeopardize his escape. This is your lucky day, Bailey, he said to himself as he turned his mount away from the corrals. Not seeking to attract attention, he rode quietly out of the town.

Scott saddled the bay horse as he too intended an exercise ride, but watched where Jarrett went to avoid taking the same route. He was just tightening his cinch when Maley came hurrying up.

'Have you seen Lije Jarrett?' he demanded.

'Sure have. He's just left – must be going for a ride. Didn't look like he intended to go far.'

'Like hell. He's running. Ashton's started talking and Jarrett's in this business up to his neck. I'm going to take one of these horses and go after him. I'll need your help.'

'Be quick. He's getting away.'

'Don't wait for me. Get on his track and follow him. Leave a clear trail that I can follow – get going.'

Scott wheeled the bay horse, touched it lightly with the spurs and set it after Jarrett, who by now was a tiny dot on the road west. As he raced past the sheriff's office, he saw Hennessey look out the door. If the lawman said anything it was lost against the sound of pounding hoofs.

For the first mile the road ran straight and it was

easy to keep his quarry in sight. After slightly narrowing the gap between them, Scott eased his mount's pace, preferring to stay well back in the hope that Jarrett would not know he was being followed. It paid to be cautious and Scott was becoming increasingly wary. As the road wound into the mountain foothills it twisted around the contours of the land with long sections screened by bends, trees and brush offering a variety of ambush sites if the packer turned at bay.

Like most fugitives Jarrett frequently looked over his shoulder and it was not long before he saw the rider on his trail. His first impulse was to attempt to outrun the pursuer, but when he saw it was only one man, he changed his mind. If he could dispose of the rider, he could gain an extra horse and make much better time by changing mounts when the ridden one tired. He had not taken a rifle when he left Crossville because he did not wish to attract undue attention so he knew he would have to get close to his victim. For all he knew the other rider might have been carrying a rifle which would give him an advantage beyond pistol range. He would need to choose his position well.

Scott knew that Jarrett had no rifle as he had seen him saddling his horse and drew some comfort from that, but when it came to handling a revolver, the fleeing man's skill was unknown. He had never considered himself more than an average handgun shot and if a confrontation took place, he could only

141

hope that Jarrett was no better. Part of him wanted to catch up with the packer and settle accounts for all time, but his cautious side told him otherwise. If he stayed on Jarrett's trail and could lead the lawmen to him, he would still have brought about the fugitive's downfall.

At a high point on the trail, Scott looked back and saw in the distance a dust cloud. It was still a couple of miles away but he knew that the lawmen were on their way.

Not far ahead Jarrett made an alarming discovery when he rounded a bend in the trail. The treeline had stopped and only barren rocky ground extended to the summit of the mountain range. He would not be able to conceal his horse and would lose the element of surprise. The options were to continue running or turn back to where concealment was better. He chose the latter and it cost him vital time.

Scott rounded a bend in the trail in time to see Jarrett barely fifty yards away urging his horse into a clump of brush on the high side of the trail. For an instant both men exchanged startled glances. Then both spurred their mounts into the closest cover capable of concealing them. Because the hampering brush slowed horses, but was too low to conceal a mounted man, each rider dismounted and sought shelter behind the granite boulders that dotted the slope.

Scott drew his gun and fired first. He did not expect to score a hit but hoped that the sound would

142

carry to Maley. The shot missed but hit a rock and whined away close to the ears of Jarrett's loose horse. The animal snorted and ran a couple of paces before it stepped on a rein and stopped out in the open.

Jarrett cursed under his breath as he would need to cross too much dangerously exposed ground to reach the animal. Now he was committed to a life-and-death contest. Given that he was facing a death penalty, surrender was not an option.

Scott knew he had time on his side. He had only to keep his opponent tied down until help arrived. If Jarrett wanted to carry the fight to him, he would have to take the greater risks. As he saw things, the packer had to launch a frontal attack or risk a run for his horse. Either way he was at a disadvantage.

A clump of weeds allowed Scott to peer from behind it, sheltering, and gave a reasonably good view of the place from which an attack could be expected. Quickly he refilled the fired chamber in his Colt, working by feel as he studied the scene before him. A slight movement in the chaparral ahead caught his eye but he resisted the urge to aim below it and shoot. He did not want to fire until he had a clear target, It would be foolish to betray his position by the cloud of powder smoke that would result, especially if a bird or small animal had caused the movement. Be patient, he told himself.

The morning was growing hotter and the sun was beating down on Jarrett as the position he had selected gave little protection from the sun. Sweat was soon trickling down his face but he was reluctant to wipe it away in case the movement betrayed his position. Scott's silence puzzled him too. Was his opponent quietly working some sort of outflanking movement? Then the idea occurred to him that lack of nerve might be behind the worrying inactivity. The notion was worth a try. 'Bailey!' he shouted. 'Do you want to make a deal?'

No reply.

'It's worth five hundred dollars to you just to let me get on my horse and ride away. I'll put the money out where you can see it. Don't risk getting your head shot off. Be sensible.'

His voice echoed around the hillside but no answer came back.

'I reckon you're scared, Bailey. This is your last chance. You have five seconds to make up your mind and then I'm coming to kill you. It don't have to be this way. You can live well for a year on that money. You'd better make up your mind pronto. I'm about to start counting and if you don't take this offer, you're dead.'

Scott moved into a crouched position, cocked his gun and looked ahead. He knew that the other was not bluffing, but Jarrett's voice also gave away his position. The packer had to break cover to carry out his threat and he did not know where his intended target was waiting. . . .

At the count of five, Jarrett allowed another couple of seconds for a last-second mind change and jumped to his feet. He moved about two paces before Scott also stood up, his feet planted firmly and looking straight at him through the sights of his revolver.

'Come on, back-shooter,' he jeered.

The taunt touched a raw nerve in Jarrett. He fired a hasty shot to panic his opponent, but anger and violent movement made a bad base for pistol shooting. The shot went wide and the bore of Scott's Colt followed his actions like an evil eye.

Jarrett was raising his gun for a more carefully aimed shot when he felt the impact of a bullet, heard the roar of the report, and saw the resulting cloud of gunsmoke. He staggered but did not fall. Struggling to retain his balance and fighting to get his breath, he raised his gun again but his movements were slow and pain had replaced shock.

Scott knew he had time and aimed carefully. As the gun kicked in his hand he saw Jarrett smashed backwards, falling to the sloping ground and rolling slightly down the incline. The gun had fallen from his hand and an expression of shock was frozen on his features. The lifeless eyes stared up at the blue sky.

Then he heard galloping horses and Maley and Macklin came pounding around the bend in the trail. They saw Scott and wheeled their foam-covered horses, halting when they reached him.

'Is that Jarrett?' Maley looked towards the body that was partially concealed by weeds.

145

'It's him. He's dead.'

Macklin dismounted. 'Did he get you at all, Scott?'

'No, I didn't give him the chance.'

The investigator dismounted and picked up the dead man's gun. He opened the loading gate and punched out the fired shell. For a second he studied the head stamp. 'Schofield ammunition – looks like we might have found the man who shot Lieutenant Cowell.'

Macklin paused in his inspection of the dead man. 'Seems like the whole gang has been wrapped up one way or another now.'

'I wouldn't be so sure,' Maley said abruptly. 'This was part of a big operation that involved other stores depots in the Department of the Missouri. Individually each operation did not seem big but when scattered through several posts, it constituted a big loss to the Quartermaster's Department. There are a few loose ends that are still worrying me.'

'So you reckon the game ain't over yet,' Macklin observed.

'I didn't say that. It could be, but I have to assess what evidence is available. I am not counting my chickens before they are hatched.'

NINETEEN

Gilmore was annoyed that the pack train's departure had been postponed again. Too many of his men were dead and it was still uncertain if Scott Bailey would be allowed to leave Crossville until Maley and the sheriff had finalized their enquiries. He was not happy about telegraphing Fort Harris to send three experienced packers to take the remaining mules and equipment to the base. He missed Jarrett's expertise for he had been a good organizer despite his newly revealed criminal habits.

In the absence of further direction, Scott had been feeding the mules and giving short rides to some recently broken to the saddle. He was the last employee that Gilmore had left. Two others had drawn their time and left town. He too was sick of Crossville and the ongoing doubts about his future employment. When he saw the contractor approaching, he waited expectantly for the news that he would deliver.

'I have a bit more news, Bailey,' Gilmore

announced. 'I've arranged for three of my men from Fort Harris to come with the wagons that will be shifting the troops and heavy stores back to the fort. When they get here, they will collect this section of the pack train and take it over the mountains to Harris. The colonel over there is a bit worried because if he has to take the field against a Cheyenne outbreak, he won't have a full pack train, so the quicker they get there, the better.'

'Where does that leave me?'

'If the law's done with you, you can come with the pack train. There's still a job for you at Fort Harris. However, I'll pay you up for the week ending when the mules move out if you still have to stay around this hole in the ground after the others are ready to go. Later there'll be a job for you if you come to Fort Harris. How does that suit you?'

'Sounds fine to me. So I just look after these Missouri jack rabbits until I know what's happening?'

'That's it. I'm heading out today. I'm looking forward to getting out with the army again.' With that announcement, Gilmore produced his wallet and pulled out a twenty-dollar bill. 'Here's an advance on the wages due to you. The new train boss will finalize the money side of it when he arrives. Best of luck, Bailey.'

Scott watched the big man walk away. Under other circumstances he would have enjoyed working for Gilmore, but as things were he had too much on his mind.

He was uneasy about Maley and his investigation and wished that it was over. The little man would appear at unexpected moments, ask questions and walk away without commenting on the replies. Sometimes he would ask questions he had asked before. Did he have a bad memory or was there a reason for his behaviour?

Wade was completing the army side of the move and Scott found that the soldier was always ready to listen to his doubts. After work they sometimes shared a drink together in what had been Gilmore's office.

'Be careful,' Wade warned as they discussed the day's events. 'Maley could be trying to trap you into contradicting yourself. He's a devious little skunk.'

'But why would he be after me? I know nothing except what happened after I arrived here. He would know I could not be mixed up in the trouble that's been going on around here. He has nothing to gain by involving me.'

'Could be he thought you were recruited by the gang or it could be something as simple as the thrill of the chase,' Wade said seriously. 'Maley trusts nobody. The more people he can drag into court, the better it looks to his bosses in Washington. He has a reputation for getting results. He is also sus-pected of making up evidence and racks up convictions like a Cheyenne brave collects scalps. If stories are right, there are a lot of innocent men in prison or even dead because of his obsession.

Everyone's a crook but him. He's a very dangerous self-promoter so don't make the mistake of trusting him.'

'Do you know that for sure?'

Wade thought for a while before answering. 'I can't tell you all I know. I would if I could, but at present I have to keep my mouth shut. Just don't trust Maley.'

Scott said suspiciously, 'Sounds like there's something I ought to know. Everyone around here seems to be keeping secrets except me. When I ask questions I get vague answers, if I get answers at all. Every man and his dog seems to be interested in what I have to say as though I know all about what's going on here.'

'Just be patient a bit longer, Scott. There are important things I can't tell you at present. I have to leave it at that.'

'Seems to me that two different parties are investigating the problems here.'

'I didn't say that,' Wade told him sharply. 'Let's leave things be for a while.'

Later, lying on his bunk and trying to sleep he reached the conclusion that he would make a few enquiries of his own.

Next morning, on the pretext of being helpful, he called at the sheriff's office and found Macklin on duty. The deputy indicated a chair and poured two cups of freshly made coffee from a pot on his desk.

'You look like a man with a load on his mind,

Scott,' he said as he passed a cup to his visitor.

Scott told him that he expected to be moving with the pack train and wanted to make sure that the legal aspects of Jarrett's death would not impede the move.

Macklin undertook to examine the paperwork relating to the case and would let him know within the next day or so. He also jokingly informed Scott to be careful as too many of the people connected to the pack train had finished up dead. 'First it was Ed Newton,' the deputy explained. 'Poor old Ed was not very important, but things got really serious when Arthur Meade got killed in that fire.'

'So you don't think Meade might have started the fire or was too drunk to know what was happening?'

'Damn sure I don't. Meade was a government investigator. He made himself known to me and Hennessey in case he needed help in a hurry. He had one of them letters that Maley was flashing around. He was not a drunk like Cowell and the others claimed he was.'

'I wonder if he was among the soldiers who were around when I started work with the pack train. Jarrett only introduced me to Cowell and another packer. I think it was Bill Ruskin but I was a bit flustered at the time. I thought I was running late when I saw the mules already packed. I know now that the pack boxes were either empty or filled with rubbish. Ed and I were not expected to come back and the loss of the packs would account for some of the shortages at the supply depot. Cowell and Jarrett must have been tipped off that the army was checking stores.'

'You spoiled everything when you survived that ambush,' Macklin said. 'Cowell and his friends were frightened by what they thought you knew or might find out. They had a couple of tries at killing you but you've been lucky. The fire at the depot destroyed the records and all stock would have been written off, including stuff that had been illegally sold. By killing Meade they thought they were safe but then Maley arrived and started asking questions. Everything fell apart then and those in the gang that weren't killed are now in jail.'

'That's good to know. Now I have to see Maley and find out if he needs me to stay here after the mules leave. Have you seen him around today?'

'Can't say I have, but he's always here somewhere. I wish he'd go back to Washington or wherever the hell he came from. His work's finished here.'

'Maybe the climate here agrees with him.'

Macklin laughed. 'He wouldn't like anything that agreed with him. I think he's just a miserable sort of cuss who's happy when he's spreading misery around.'

'I think you're being a bit hard on him. I know he's not the friendliest person I've met but I've seen a lot worse.'

'He didn't get his reputation by being kind to people. Don't ever make the mistake of thinking he's your friend.'

TWENTY

Scott was about to return to the mule corral when Mary Hegarty came down the street on her black pony. He stepped off the boardwalk to intercept her. She saw him and halted her mount beside him.

'Scott,' she said. 'I'm glad I caught you. I thought you might have moved out.'

'It could be a couple of days yet. We're waiting for a wagon and some packers who are coming with it. That's if the law lets me go. I might be wanted around here for a while yet. Anyone would think I had the answers to all their questions.'

'Do you really want to go with the pack train?'

'It's a job, Mary. I haven't been able to find any cattle work.'

The girl's face brightened. 'Would you be interested in working for us?'

'I would be, but your ranch is not very big. Do you really need an extra hand?'

She replied, 'We need someone to represent us at

the fall roundup. We have about sixty head of cows and an unknown number of calves running on the open range and want to be sure that the right brand goes on them. It will only be temporary work, but you will get to know a lot of the bigger ranchers and there's a good chance one of them might offer you a job. What do you think?'

'It sounds pretty good to me. Would it be OK with your folks?'

'Pa told me to make the offer. He'll pay you what you are getting now and you'll find that the grub and housing are a lot better than you will get with a pack train traipsing around the mountains somewhere. You can start when you finish here and will be on our payroll until the roundup's over and Pa decides what cattle he wants to sell.'

Scott knew that under the circumstances he was unlikely to receive a better offer. 'Sounds good to me. I'll start making arrangements now so I can quit as soon as the new packers arrive.'

They talked for a few more minutes, but each had other tasks to perform, so reluctantly they went their separate ways.

Scott was hurrying back to the mule corrals to ensure that the animals had feed and water. With Gilmore gone he was the sole packer left at the depot and envisaged a couple of busy days before the others arrived. Turning a corner, he saw Maley ahead, just entering the shed that the soldiers were using as a temporary office.

He had been wondering where the investigator had been, but was not surprised that the little man was keeping close contact with Wade, who was now in charge of the few troops left. Casually he strolled towards the shed, rehearsing in his mind the announcement that he was quitting.

The sound of the shot came as a complete surprise. Another followed before the first echoes had died away and then he heard a third report.

Without thinking he drew his gun and ran to the shed. The smell of burnt powder hung heavy in the air as he came through the door and stepped sideways to avoid making an easy target in the bright light of the opening. His foot struck something on the floor and a gun slid across the boards.

Wade was standing with a drawn gun and Maley was on the floor. The soldier swung his weapon towards Scott but made no attempt to fire.

'Wade, what's happening?'

'Maley tried to kill me, but I got him first.'

'Why would he do that?'

'Because I'm a special investigator for the army. Maley's the head of the gang who've been selling army stores. He's not a government man at all.'

Scott was not convinced. 'But why would he be here? Wouldn't he be running?'

'He was here to get rid of the evidence and possible witnesses. He's the head of this whole operation. I have enough on that slimy little skunk to hang him six times over but I've saved Uncle Sam the trouble.'

'Don't believe him, Bailey.' The voice from the man on the floor was weak but the words were chilling. 'He'll kill you as soon as you drop your guard.'

'So you're still alive,' Wade said in surprise. 'You're tougher than I thought, but you still lie the same as ever. Now shut your damn mouth and die in peace.'

Keeping a close eye on the corporal, Scott spoke warily. 'Keep talking, Maley. The law will be here soon and they can sort things out. Right now I'm not sure whom to trust.'

'Don't be a fool, Bailey.' Maley's voice was now only a whisper but was made stronger by its urgent tone. 'He'll kill us both before the sheriff arrives.'

Wade lifted his gun. 'Still the lying swine you always were, Maley. Don't listen to him, Scott. I've always played straight with you. Remember I told you that I couldn't tell you all that was going on? I was trying to lure this coyote out and it worked. He came in here trying to kill me.'

'Don't trust him. . . .' Maley's voice was becoming weaker. 'He has to kill us both before Hennessey arrives.'

Scott had not holstered his gun and was holding it, still cocked in his hand. It took only a slight movement to cover the corporal. 'Drop the gun, Wade.'

'Why should I? You forget I'm a federal officer.'

'If you drop your gun, Sheriff Hennessey can check the claims of both of you without anyone else getting hurt. Maley's not going anywhere. There's no—'

Scott had no time to finish what he was saying before he saw the soldier's gun swing towards him. Without hesitation, he squeezed the trigger. The report sounded like a cannon in the confined space. He saw Wade reel, but recover quickly. He was jumping sideways when the soldier's gun roared.

No bullet struck him and through a cloud of powder smoke, Scott fired again. Wade's shot came almost simultaneously but the shooter was already falling and that slug, too, missed its mark.

Before he hit the floor, the corporal hit the wall behind him and he fell sideways to land in a crumpled heap with his gun still clutched in his hand.

'Be careful of him,' Maley gasped.

'No need to. He's hit fair and square and he's dead.'

A clatter of boots came from outside and the two lawmen charged through the door, the sheriff holding a sawn-off shotgun.

'Drop that gun, Bailey, then tell me what's going on here.'

'Wade shot Maley. He needs a doctor quick, if he's still alive.'

'I'll get him,' Macklin said, and hurried out the door again.

'Who shot Wade?'

'I did. He was fixing to kill the pair of us. He might have succeeded in Maley's case. We'd better see what we can do for him.'

The wounded man stirred. Struggling for breath,

he gasped, 'Be quick . . . about it. Too many people
. . . will be happy . . . if I die. Don't want that.'

Hennessey knelt beside the prostrate man. 'Where
are you hit?'

'S-side . . . ribs feel broken. Might be hit in the
lung.'

'Ain't your lung,' the sheriff told him. 'I seen a few
men shot there. Mostly they were half drowning in
their own blood. The doctor should be here soon.
Macklin will find him. I know he's in town because I
saw him in the street about half an hour ago.'

Scott had three busy days helping the replacement
packers and loading the mules with the last of the
train's equipment. By the time the remaining three
soldiers had boarded the wagon to return by road to
Fort Harris, he had been paid and had time on his
hands again. Anxious to clear any legal matters that
might keep him in Crossville, he called in to the
sheriff's office. Both lawmen were there.

'Howdy, gents,' he greeted. 'Any word on how
Maley's doing?'

'He'll live,' Hennessey muttered. 'He got hit twice
but neither of the bullets hit anything vital. I saw him
this morning. He'll be living in the doctor's spare
room till he's fit to travel.'

Macklin laughed. 'I wonder what the doctor's wife
thinks of that. He's not the brightest company.'

'He's not,' Scott agreed. 'But I don't think he's as
bad as people say. What I saw of him, he was a

straight dealer. That's why I took his word over Wade's.'

Hennessey looked puzzled. 'That's the bit I don't understand. You liked Wade, most people did, so why did you side with Maley?'

'Something Wade said jogged my memory. He said he had always been straight with me. I remembered then that he had told me that Meade fella who was killed in the fire was a drunk. Other people who knew him said otherwise so I figured he was lying.'

'Turns out he was, but it was mighty slim evidence to shoot a man on. Lots of folks tell lies.'

'I had to decide quick because Wade knew you would be coming and he could not afford to leave either of us alive. I am still wondering, though, how a corporal could be running such a big swindle with so many officers about. Had he originally been taking orders from Lieutenant Cowell?'

'Not according to Maley,' the sheriff explained. 'He reckoned that the criminals had been operating from several army posts and stores. There were some officers involved, but not all were willing participants so the thieves recruited only those they could black-mail. They picked their marks: gamblers, embezzlers, drunks, people of dubious morals, there's no short-age of such types in the army. It was easier to turn a blind eye and play along with some minor misdeeds than to have a career ruined. Once an officer had been recruited and the officer committed one crimi-nal act, he was their prisoner. By day the officers gave the orders, but when nobody was around, the criminals took over. Maley reckoned that Cowell was about to crack and spill the beans and that's why Jarrett shot him. Suicides are common at army posts where there are so many heavy drinkers.'

'So it's all over now?'

Hennessey nodded. 'For us it is. What are your plans?'

'I have work at the Hegarty ranch until after the fall roundup and hope to pick up another job then – and just while I think of it, is there any chance I can buy that bay horse I've been riding?'

'Sure can. I have the job of selling off the effects of some criminals you helped put in the boneyard. Any money goes towards the funeral costs. If you have ten dollars the horse is yours.'

Scott was not sure he had heard right. 'Ten dollars – are you sure? That's awful cheap.'

'I'd give him to you, but you need some legal claim. You helped us a lot and only got packer's pay for it. Hand over ten bucks and I'll write a receipt. Then I reckon you'll be riding hard for the Hegarty place. Mary must be getting anxious about you.'

Scott suddenly looked embarrassed. 'What makes you think that she would worry?'

Macklin laughed loudly. 'This is a small town, Scott. Everyone knows everyone else's business. Now get going before someone else comes in and makes a better offer for that horse.'